CW01020692

WITHIN THE WIND, BENEATH THE SNOW

A SNOWBOOKS HORROR NOVELLA

Proudly published by Snowbooks

Copyright © 2016 Ray Cluley

Snowbooks Ltd.
email: info@snowbooks.com
www.snowbooks.com.

British Library Cataloguing in Publication Data.
A catalogue record for this book is available
from the British Library.

Paperback: 978-1-911390-87-9
Ebook: 978-1-911390-86-2

For Simon and Cate
Beware the dottooth!

Ray Cluley

xx

WITHIN THE WIND,
BENEATH THE SNOW

R<small>AY</small> C<small>LULEY</small>

ACKNOWLEDGEMENTS

First of all, many thanks go to Snowbooks for doing such a bloody wonderful job with this book. You've been an absolute pleasure to work with and your whole range of novellas has been beautifully produced - I couldn't be happier.

As for the writing of the material...

Peter Tennant used to run an advent calendar event that encouraged flash fiction from a variety of writers, and much of the bonus material here first appeared as a result of those challenges. So thank you, Pete.

Thanks are due to Michael Wilson, too, who first published 'The Rain Deer' online at This is Horror. Thanks, man, and keep up the great work.

Sigur Rós, thank you for the music. I wrote 'Within the Wind, Beneath the Snow' with a playlist of your albums on repeat. Inspirational and evocative, as always.

Finally, a great big thank you goes to Jess Jordan, who motivates me, encourages me, and in various ways helps me create my best work. Jess, you keep the darkteeth quiet and the cold at bay and I thank you forever with a hand over one eye.

And now, on with the stories. As M. R. James once wrote, "If they serve to amuse some readers at the Christmas-time that is coming – or at any time whatever – they will justify my action in publishing them."

RAY CLULEY, 2016

WITHIN THE WIND, BENEATH THE SNOW

Dog star.

"It is the brightest star in the heavens."

Gjerta Jørgensen was dreaming and she was remembering. She was a girl, hearing her father's voice.

"It is called Sirius."

Gjerta wanted to nod, to say, "Yes Papa," but the part that was a girl also knew that she was a woman sleeping, a woman trying to not wake up, not yet. A woman trying to not hear the wind as it howled outside the tent, howled like –

"The Dog Star."

Gjerta remembered looking but seeing no dog. Her father crouched beside her.

"And that's where we go, Papa?"

Her father, already holding her close and pointing to the sky, held her even closer and said, "Yes. That is where we go."

Gjerta had nodded then as a girl and her Papa's beard tickled her face. She nodded in the dream as well, though part of her could hear the wind now, and the sound it carried within.

When she woke she immediately felt the cold. Felt it bite beneath her skin and scrape the heat from her bones.

*

"Twenty two miles."

Gjerta nodded, though she doubted they would cover so much ground in one day. Not with only twelve dogs. Losing Lykee had

1

made more of a difference than they had expected. They missed her more than the radio.

Søren Olsen knew these thoughts. He nodded back at her and amended the distance. "Nineteen." He was anxious; they were already overdue.

Gjerta nodded and said nothing else. They ate their steaming breakfast, drank very hot coffee, and listened to the dogs outside turning on their chains and chuffing occasionally at the wind. The only light came from the stoves that had cooked their breakfast; they'd left them on for the warmth. The stove-light showed how dark it was around them, how it pressed against the tent from outside.

"Twenty," Gjerta said. She was eager, as well, to get back.

Søren grunted and patted her shoulder. "I will see to the dogs."

*

When Gjerta was ten years old, her father took her into the woods at night to teach her there was more to them than what you could see in the day. At first, Gjerta had been afraid of the woods at night. She never told her father but she thought he knew. That was why he did it. Not because he was a cruel man but because he wanted her unafraid. Some parts of the forest were truly dark, the trees leaning close or reaching out to others with limbs as long as promises and laden with heavy snow. In these places you were guided by the sounds of the world around you, the hard scrunch of slow footsteps in the snow, the shudder of snow knocked from lower branches, the route the wind took around and through the pines, carrying the snow, shifting the snow. Always snow. The woods were alive with sound at night. Pine trunks expanded with the cold. An unseen animal sniffed for its prey or predator. Occasionally Gjerta saw things in the dark, but the sounds frightened her more.

"You have heard these things before," Papa said, "but you could see, so you did not listen. Now you cannot see. You do not need to see these things to know they are there, and that they cannot harm you. You know the animals here. You know the trees. I have felt you beside me turn or crouch to avoid branches you could not see, and you have moved around tree stumps; how did you know they were there?"

Gjerta did not have an answer for him because she did not know she'd done these things.

"You felt them there. You smelt the sap, the bark, the leaf, felt the breath of the wind upon them and past them. You heard it, felt it, and so you saw it without seeing."

And like what Papa had said about the trees, Gjerta felt him smile in the dark when he said, "Do you see?" as a sort of joke.

"Yes, Papa."

"When you can see, that is all you do. The night is better. When you can't see, you see better."

"Yes, Papa."

Gjerta, though, knew her father more than she knew the woods. If Gjerta ducked, it was because she felt the wind on her when Papa stopped blocking it. She knew to stand again because she smelt the sweat of her father and the musk of his animal pelts as he rose up before her. A sudden chill told her to move because her father had, and she paused when the warmth ahead seemed closer. Eventually Gjerta knew the woods at night, but she knew them through knowing her father.

She could never tell him about the other sounds, though. He didn't hear them. Sometimes they were words, and that was all right because she knew the voice, but sometimes there was only the biting cold and the sound of its hunger. It hid inside the wind, in the shadows, beneath the snow, and when it spoke its voice had no words but Gjerta heard them all the same. It said it was coming, it was always coming, and she would never be ready even though it warned her.

*

Gjerta hacked at the ice that had formed around the runners, careful not to damage them. She kept her movements slight and slow. Patience and careful consideration were key survival skills out here. A lapse of concentration and something was broken or someone was hurt or the wind took something precious like a hat, a glove, a map. Or a radio was somehow lost.

Søren was harnessing the dogs. She could hear his gruff commands and their barked excitement. The wind snapped the sounds around so that the dark was filled with them and the chit... chit...chit of her steady chipping, counting time to a crescendo she had come to love.

"Ya!"

Then the pull of the traces, taut and sudden, as sled and man and woman lurched violently forward to race across the snow.

Gjerta and Søren had built the sled together. It had been part of their training, bonding them as partners, providing an understanding essential for any repair and creating a sense of ownership that increased the extent to which they valued an already prized piece of equipment. Nearly fifteen feet in length, it had runners made of nylon and boards fastened together not with nails but with twine because it gave them more flexibility on the hard packed ice and snow. They painted it black and afterwards Gjerta won the right to name it. "Nothing girly," Søren said. She named it the Morten Pine. Morten was a saint's name, but she'd had to explain it to Søren.

"Morten gave half of his cloak to a beggar so that he might live through the winter."

They had been at Daneborg at the time, warm within the blocky buildings of headquarters, but they knew how much colder it would become as they travelled north to Danmarkshavn. They were waiting for the frozen sea ice to thicken, but they'd had the whiteout of a blizzard twice already, finding their way between buildings thanks to permanent guide ropes connecting them. Soon they would be making a six-hundred-and-ninety-mile journey, travelling almost as far north as Greenland could take them, and there would be no guide ropes there.

"We'll need more than half a cloak, Jørgensen," Søren said. He always called her by her surname. She wondered if it was because calling her Gjerta was to admit she was a woman.

Gjerta was not only the first woman Slædepatruljen Sirius had taken, she was the first to even apply. It had surprised her, even as tough as the job was. She couldn't believe that no other woman had tried to be a part of such a prestigious elite unit, to rise to the challenges it offered. Sirius was the world's only military dogsled team, responsible for patrolling more than eight thousand miles of Greenland's north-east coast, the largest national park in the world and one of the least hospitable places on Earth. Six teams patrolled the coastline over a five year service, each member pushed to the limits of hunger and exhaustion, risking frostbite and attack. The risks weren't only physical; as beautiful as Greenland could be, the desolation of it, the isolation, could torture a weak mind. The pay was terrible, there were no holidays at all, and you travelled with no one but each other and thirteen dogs to call company. Perhaps they'd meet a herd of musk oxen. Perhaps polar bears, though she hoped not. Northeast Greenland had no permanent population. The Danish missionaries and colonists who came in the eighteenth century lived on the west coast. The north east was too cold, too barren. The average temperature was twenty five below zero and could drop to as low as minus seventy. Half a cloak certainly would not do.

"Ya!"

The wind pushed at them as they sped into it.

Some of the others travelled light to travel fast; Jesper and Niels even cut the handles from their toothbrushes. They said they cut the labels from their clothes, too, and though Gjerta thought they were joking, they might not have been. Gjerta and Søren, on the other hand, overloaded the Morten Pine and travelled slow, skiing alongside. They carried food for themselves and the dogs, stoves, fuel, tents, sleeping gear, first aid kit, maps, rifles. Gjerta and Søren needed everything on their sled, all eight hundred pounds of it.

The radio, though, was lost. They had looked for it. The terrain was rocky and often strewn with broken stone, with sheer slopes and sudden drops where the tundra was split into fissures, but they checked as well as they could in what light they had. It had been a tense time, Søren saying very little but surely blaming her for its loss. They did not find it. In December, five hundred miles north of the Arctic Circle, it was dark twenty four hours a day. The shoreline was little more than a paleness between the night sky and the sea, and they only had the lights of their headlamps to guide them. They saw their last sunset in the early days of their journey, and after that the days became darker and darker, although never quite completely. They lived in a world that varied in shades of grey. A forever solstice of perpetual twilight. The ground was incandescent with the shine of stars and moon-silver; all the dark did was hold the light down to stop it escaping.

*

"Look. It is never really dark, not completely. Look." Papa crouched down beside her, leant in close, and pointed up at where the sky peeked through a gap in the trees. "Stars," he said.

Troels Jørgensen traced the patterns of the stars for his daughter, joining them, and Gjerta saw that the stars were not separate, that the darkness around them held lines that couldn't be seen because they were so far away. She learned the powers of the constellations. The stars would always show her the right way.

To test his daughter's new knowledge, Troels took Gjerta deeper into the woods than he ever had before. They stopped frequently and he would ask her, "Which way home?" Gjerta was proud to be right every time. She understood the darkness of the sky.

But the dark between the trees was different. Gjerta could not explain this to Papa. She did not have the right words for it. The darkness between the trees had teeth you couldn't see until they were upon you. Not fox teeth, not wolf, nor the teeth of a bear.

Darkteeth.

Gjerta knew they were there. She could hear them.

She had first heard them on the night her mother walked away, her red coat disappearing into the dark between the trees...

"Papa, look."

A small cabin stood in the darkness, so deep amongst the trees that it appeared to grow there. Its roof seemed to be made entirely of the branches and leaves of neighbouring spruce, and the timber of its walls had clothed itself green so that a small single window was set in moss. The door was only known to them because it was open slightly, a slice of darkness deeper than the night and starless.

"Trapper's lodge," said Papa. He pointed to wooden frames nearby where pelts had once hung. "An old one, from the looks of it. Come on, I will show you."

He went ahead. Gjerta could follow, as was expected, or wait where skins had been stretched across frames and scraped clean. She fancied she could hear the ghosts of them, thrumming taut as the wind passed, crying out at the darkteeth that had claimed them.

She followed her father.

He struggled with the door. Time and climate had warped the wood, changed its shape. He tugged it with both hands then set his shoulder to it. It protested with stuttering grunts but eventually opened for them and he went in, into the dark.

For a moment Gjerta feared the door would snap shut, trapping her father inside, trapping her outside, but it didn't.

Again, she followed him.

The cabin smelled damp, rich with the wet smell of forest. Her father produced a torch from his pocket and swept the light around the single room. Pine needles made a carpet under their feet so that they stepped around in silence, releasing a sweet aroma with every crush of their feet. Foliage crept in through a large hole in the roof, the debris of its collapse scattered amongst the leaves and piled into one ruined corner of the room. There was a table, with a kerosene lamp standing at its centre. Papa picked it up and shook it and set it down again. There was a wooden chair, and a bed that had slumped at one edge.

Beside it was a crouching shape. Gjerta clutched her father's arm.

"It's not what you think," he told her, pulling away from his daughter's grip but holding her afterwards. "Look."

The bear was dead. Closer, Gjerta saw it wasn't a bear at all, though it once had been. It was a rug, rolled and bunched into a loose crouch that still had its claws, and an open-mouthed head that still had its —

"Careful."

"Papa!"

But he held her firm, gripping her shoulders. Gjerta had nearly stepped into a hole in the floor, a darkness amongst the darkness. She would have fallen barely half a metre, but as her father had often said, the consequences of any action could be serious if help was too far to come when called.

He crouched and found the open trapdoor buried beneath the dry pine needles. He raised it, and lowered it closed. He stood upon it to show it was safe and looked up to where a beam above still dangled a short length of rope. He amended his earlier assessment of the place.

"Poacher's lodge," he said.

"What's the rope for, Papa?" She feared the answer but asked anyway.

He told her, "Not what you think."

But still Gjerta stared, and so he explained how poachers would skin their kills inside, out of sight, and the trapdoor in the floor was so the blood dripped to the ground beneath instead of the floor. Then the meat and the furs and any trophy they might want could be stored beneath, in the cold, like in a larder. The trapdoor, when it was closed, would be hidden by a rug.

"Because people like you come and check?"

"Yes. They hide things because of people like me."

"But you didn't know this place was here."

Her father looked around as if deciding whether this was true.

"If it's a poacher's lodge, why are there skinning frames outside?" Gjerta asked.

He had no answer for her.

"Come on," he said. "Let's see if you can find the way back."

*

They were travelling at approximately six miles per hour. It was fast for the terrain; there was a depot hut en route they were pushing for. Not only did they want its supplies but they were eager to sleep somewhere with walls that weren't canvas. Even the dogs were eager to cover a lot of ground, pulling ahead with little complaint. They liked to run. Gjerta liked to run with them.

"Twenty miles," Søren called. He shouted to be heard over the wind and the rushing sound of snow beneath their skis, the constant shush of the sled between them.

Gjerta was windmilling first one arm, then the other, in an effort to maintain a good circulation and to keep warm, but she stopped briefly to offer Søren a thumbs up. Søren paused in his own arm circles to return the gesture. On this terrain, if the weather was against them, they could spend an entire day on the move and travel no more than a single mile. There had been many days like that. At the moment, though, they were travelling offshore whenever they could, the frozen sea free of rocks that might trouble them, though still treacherous in ways of its own. They didn't begin their patrol until the ice was thick enough for travel, but nevertheless, even with winter, Gjerta worried it was too thin. Here, if they weren't careful, they risked plunging into ice cold water, dark and hidden beneath the surface. Their training may have prepared them for the shock of a cold swim and what to do afterwards, but they'd lose the tethered dogs and everything on the sled, not to mention the sled itself. They would die without it.

The dogs were grey black blurs on the ice ahead, kicking up clouds of snow and leaving puffs of breath behind them. Occasionally there was the tang of urine as they relieved themselves on the run. Gjerta and Søren yelled their encouragement and reprimands, the ever-changing mixture of praise and persuasion that made up their constant interaction with the dogs. Each had been trained almost as hard as Gjerta and Søren and they worked tirelessly.

They were useful in other ways, too. Hagen, who would be the alpha without Gjerta and Søren, knew which fissures in the ice the sled could manage and which ones had to be avoided, stopping before a drop they could not see. Poncho was always the first to sense a polar bear, warning them with a strange sound that was only part growl. Valkyrie was the expert sled dog, close to matching the record for years in service. She was certainly the longest serving female: nine years, nearly twice the usual term. Valkyrie was one of Gjerta's favourites, along with Voksen. You weren't supposed to have any, it could ruin the family dynamic, so she was careful not to show it.

"Ya!"

To the right, broken rock and monolithic stone gradually became mountains. To the left, icebergs rose from the water like pale reflections of them, rugged shapes that were all strange lines and abrupt angles. Everything was the colour of starlight. And all between was nothing but wind and snow, offspring of the cold and dark.

Wind and snow. It was all they rushed towards, and it was all they left behind them.

*

It was light when Gjerta and her Papa started looking for the tree, but dark before they found it. Each had picked out several, but the other had disagreed every time with a shrug or wrinkled nose and they had passed by, looking. It had to be one they both felt was right.

An entire forest, and they couldn't find a tree.

The tradition had been the same for years—the pagans first, bringing trees inside to decorate for the winter solstice.

"They believed these trees were magical."

"Why, Papa?"

"Because they are evergreen. They do not die."

After the pagans, the tree became a Christian symbol at Christmas, draped with ribbons and wooden toys. But for Gjerta and her Papa, it was more than that. They always chose a tall tree, a perfect tree, and set it in front of their cabin home to decorate. Bringing one inside felt wrong somehow.

They circled the house, widening their search in an ever-growing spiral so they covered a lot of ground without travelling far from home.

"This one?"

Gjerta could tell he didn't really think so. He only suggested it because it was late. He still had to chop it down and then the two of them had to drag it home on their small sled.

"Your mother would have found the right one like this." He clicked his fingers, and smiled.

"Papa!"

She added nothing else. She didn't know if she was protesting or exclaiming her surprise. Perhaps she was doing both.

The search for the perfect Christmas tree was part of a tradition Mama had started. She always knew the right one, the perfect one, finding it within the first hour of searching. Gjerta and her Papa had continued the tradition thinking of this but never speaking of it. It had become a tradition of their own, the silence, and now Papa had broken it. They weren't really looking for a tree. Papa had made that clear by mentioning her.

Gjerta often saw her Mama walking beside them in the forest. She glimpsed her between the trees or heard her in the wind as she made snow-muffled steps ahead of them. Wrapped up in her furs and breathing on her mittened hands because she never could get them warm enough, Mama would point at a tree by nodding at it.

"There," said Gjerta.

"There," her Papa agreed.

He took the axe from his belt and passed it to her. Gjerta always made the first cuts. She would strike the trunk until she had a decent wedge of wood out and then her father would take over, passing the axe back when they were ready for the final bite.

"You do it this year," Gjerta offered. She always offered. And just like every year, her father put his hands upon her and turned her around to face the tree and said, "Maybe next year is my turn."

Every tree made the same sound at the end; a short screech and a succession of splitting and snapping that seemed to echo long after the thunder of its fall. Papa told her that the echo was the other trees telling the forest what had happened.

"It's their way of remembering."

Gjerta had often wondered if they'd prefer not to but she never asked him. Instead, she helped drag the tree home as night darkened. Back at the cabin, with the tree secured outside, they would load its limbs with candled starlight and watch how it shone and glittered, a large foil star at the top glistening in the light they'd made.

*

With the darkness came more wind and more snow. As the nights became longer, so did the storms, flurries that struck them sideways coming in off the sea, and from the front as they rushed into it. Visibility was poor, so they were careful, but they travelled faster than they should, putting their trust in the dogs to read the land ahead. The dogs paid the weather little heed; all they wanted to do was run.

Gjerta often saw faces in the snow but had learned to ignore them. Sometimes they came at her with the wind-driven snow, sometimes they rose out of the snow on the ground, open mouths set to swallow them. So when she saw a sudden shape in the gloom ahead she was tempted to ignore that, too. It was little more than an outline the snow moved around, but it was something. It was not a rock. It crouched. There was a sound, as well, buried in the howling of the wind.

Gjerta yelled a warning and steered them sharply out of the way.

They passed nothing.

Søren's headlamp cut a line to her through diagonal stripes of snow and she waved it off before he could ask.

"Fine," she yelled. "We're fine."

When Søren turned back he yelled a command to the dogs and tugged the sled into another tight turn.

Gjerta heard something snap and suddenly the sled veered hard. She was shoved down by the tightness of the turn, rolling in a jumble of skis and poles in the wake of it. Søren, across from her on the other side of the sled, was knocked sprawling, disappearing somewhere into the white dark of fast falling snow, a slashing line of light from his headlamp and then nothing.

Gjerta called out for the dogs to stop before she'd finished rolling, her skis tossing up a sharp spray of snow and ice. She called again. Only after hearing the shush of the sled runners cease did she call to Søren.

His reply was a sharp curse. He was okay.

Gjerta patted her legs from the ankles up, embraced herself to check her arms, and thought she was all right too. They had both fallen before. They had fallen lots of times. She pulled herself up with the support of a ski pole and shuffled on one ski to find the

15

other, clipping it back on with another call for Søren. Then she went to the sled. A red light blinked, calling her to it.

She called to the rearmost dogs. She couldn't see them.

"Hjørdis! Agvald!"

She was shoving hard on her skis, shouting again, as Agvald emerged from the snow he had burrowed into, fanning his tail against it and rolling to cool down now they had stopped running. Hjørdis was slower in emerging but he was there. Where else would they be?

"Jørgensen!" Søren called.

Gjerta pulled her scarf away from her mouth and felt the loss of its warmth immediately. Her breath was sharp and thin, cold spikes of air with each inhalation. She wished she could grow a beard. She called to Søren that she was okay and whistled like she would to the dogs to let him know where she was. The only death to have ever occurred in Sirius had been when partners became separated from each other during a storm. She often found herself thinking of that as she tried to sleep, what it must have felt like, alone in the dark and the cold, nothing but the wind around you and the snow beneath. Nothing but you.

"The Pine?" Søren called.

He was beating snow and ice from his furred hat as he approached. He pulled it down tight and put the hood of his jacket up over it.

"It's fine."

"What happened?"

She shrugged as best she could under her layers, knowing he would still somehow see the gesture. Each of them was as used to the other as the dogs. "What did you see?" she asked.

"See? I saw nothing."

"You turned us."

"I turned us back on course. What did you see?"

Gjerta chose not to answer that. "I heard something snap," she said.

They checked the sled but found nothing outwardly wrong; she sat true on her runners and the equipment hadn't shifted. They checked it carefully.

"The dogs."

The pair of them moved up the traces, one either side, checking a dog each as they went.

A growl and whine came from further up, sounds so close together they overlapped, and at first Søren thought it was Poncho; Gjerta could tell, because he hesitated as if to go back for the rifle. But what they heard was not Poncho's polar bear warning. It was only a whimper now. It was—

"Major!"

Gjerta dropped to her knees beside the dog. It lay curled into a ball of fur and had emptied its bladder without righting itself. Gjerta pulled her hood down and the headlamp off, pulled her face mask up. With one hand she shielded her face from the blown snow while the other held the lamp close to the dog. It looked at her with eyes that were dark and deep, all pupil even in the light of the headlamp. Before she could press for injuries she saw the snow darken. A steaming crimson upon the white. The dog whimpered. Gjerta put her hand to the dog's hind quarters and it gave a brief howl.

"Quiet, girl. Good girl."

Gjerta gently raised one of the dog's legs—

"Good girl."

—and saw that the other beneath was bent at a broken angle.

She couldn't see bone but she knew it was exposed because of the blood. The dog whimpered, and one paw kicked feebly at the snow around its muzzle.

"It is Voksen," said Søren.

"Her leg is broken."

"You called her Major. We don't have a Major."

Gjerta did not look at him. "Her leg is broken."

Søren, standing over her, tapped her arm with the butt of the rifle. He had gone back for it. He had known what the howl meant and dogs did not retire from Sirius.

Gjerta took the rifle from him and stood. Søren had done it last time, and Voksen was one of Gjerta's favourites.

"I will take the others," he said. Gjerta nodded and unfastened the harness from Voksen, hushing her when she made noises of pain. When she was free of the traces, Søren led the others away. He did not go far because of the visibility. It was more of a courtesy for Gjerta than out of any concern for the dogs.

Gjerta paused only briefly to rub at the dog's muzzle, eager to put an end to her pain. She stood and raised the rifle. "It was not your time," she said, and yet she fired.

The crack of the shot was muffled by the wind, torn quickly into pieces, and cast away across the ice and snow. But it still felt sharp enough to bite. She would hear its echo for a long time.

She stabbed at the ground with the butt of the rifle, sinking the stock into snow. She dragged an oval trench around the dog but found nothing. The shape she had made, Voksen curled within it, looked like an eye. It wept a single tear of blood that froze upon the tundra.

Gjerta shouldered the rifle, crouched, and retrieved Voksen from the snow. She carried her back to the Morten Pine.

*

"What is it, Papa?"

They were looking at a large shape in the snow. Her father had grabbed her arm hard enough to bruise it for days. He would not let go.

"Papa?"

She hadn't noticed it at first. She had been looking at the trees, trying to find the one with the best spread of branches. She was looking for the most balanced tree, very straight, with a point fit for a star and branches that fattened as they descended. A green teardrop of a tree. She had not been looking where she walked. She did not know she needed to.

A carpet of pine needles too neat to have fallen naturally waited ahead and her Papa had grabbed her arm to pull her away from it. Now they knelt together in the snow and he pointed at a slight rise beneath, an oval ridge all the way around amongst the pine needles. He put a gloved hand to the ground and swept away the leaves and snow to show her triangles of black metal. They poked from the snow like tiny flat mountains, a long crescent ridge of them. He brushed more snow away. On the other side, another crescent. He was swearing now, quietly, under his breath, but she could hear the words.

"Papa?"

"Mantrap," he said.

"What is it for?"

"It is a bad thing. It is not allowed."

Gjerta could tell he was angry even before he struck at the ground with the axe handle. Teeth snapped shut as angry punctuation, a sharp and savage sound that would forever haunt her dreams. It was the only thing she ever hated him for; nothing else had been his fault. He was not quick enough to yank the axe away and though its handle held, part of it split. Gjerta turned away and raised her hands with short scream of surprise, but she caught the splinter across her cheek, beneath her eye.

"I am sorry," her father said, tugging off his gloves to pull gently at the splinter in her cheek. "I am sorry."

She had heard him say the same things to Mama. He caressed her face when the splinter was gone, looking into her eyes as if willing her not to cry, and she had seen him do that, too.

"It's all right," he said. "You'll be all right." And those words were just for her. He had never said them before.

Gjerta didn't know why she cried. The splinter had not hurt.

Her father gathered up a length of chain from the snow. It led to a tree trunk nearby. "Go home," he told her, pulling at the trap, gathering it to him. "Go back exactly the way we came. I will take care of this. Follow our tracks and go back."

But the tracks did not go back home. They went back to the old lodge. She followed them, wondering if they were going to stay there again, wondering if Papa would come for her or if he would forget and go home.

*

Søren turned to face Gjerta, signalling with one hand while dazzling her momentarily with his headlamp. The hood of her coat limited her vision so that she had to turn her upper body to see where he pointed.

The building was a small bunkhouse, very old and so snow-laden it was as white as the ground it rose from. Gjerta was surprised he had seen it. There were few such buildings on their routes. There were several Sirius depots where they could re-supply but this wasn't one of theirs. It would do, though.

She let go of the Morten Pine, turned her skis, and grabbed again for the rope at the rear of the sled as Søren urged the dogs to turn inland. She pulled to slow their approach. She tried not to look at the bundle wrapped in tarpaulin at the rear of the sled. She tried not to think of Voksen.

Søren turned, dazzling her again briefly to offer an OK signal. He was not thinking of the dead dog. He was probably grinning but it was impossible to see behind the face mask and goggles. Gjerta nodded. She was as eager as he was to sleep in a bed, surrounded by walls that didn't shift in the wind.

In front of the cabin a pole had been staked upright into the frozen ground. The dogs sniffed at it as they passed and a couple tried to piss against it as they went but were tugged back into line by the limits of their traces. Gjerta pulled them to a standstill and turned sideways on her skis, sending up a fantail of snow. The ground around the pole was yellow now, sparkling already as the urine froze, but the ancient rust colour of very old blood still stained the stake. It was a bait stick for luring polar bears. They were attracted to upright shapes in a land that had few of them, especially when there was a slab of meat skewered on one end. Gjerta stabbed around it with her ski pole, checking for teeth.

Søren skied to the shelter. He would check inside and then unload what they needed. It was Gjerta's turn to see to the dogs. Feeding was the best way to establish a bond and the dogs had to see both of them as leaders.

21

She set the stakes in place, hammering them into the frozen ground. Then she unfastened the first, Hagen, and grabbed him under the forelegs. It was the only way to move them, else they would drag you around or, more frustrating, sit down and refuse to budge. With only the use of his back legs Hagen was unbalanced and more easily manoeuvred. She hefted him away from the sled and tethered him, repeating the process for the others, setting them apart from each other. Their team was mostly siblings, supposedly to minimise fights, but Søren, who had two brothers and a sister, had laughed at such an idea and so they kept them apart. She kept them close to the cabin, though. These were dogs that would never know the indoors, but she liked to shelter them partially from the winds and keeping them close also meant they were alerted of any danger. She went back to the sled for their food as they licked the snow from their feet; the cold could open sores, and even if it didn't the snow needed to be cleared from between the toes before it could freeze solid and cause them pain. When the dogs were done cleaning their feet, Gjerta tossed them frozen chunks of walrus. As they ate, she buried Voksen in the snow, then she kicked at the bait pole, alternating sides until it was loose enough to pull free and discard. Afterwards, she went inside.

*

The forest ground was hard with frost and unyielding to the blade of her shovel. The soil was solid, just as she knew it would be, but she struck and scraped and hoped. She didn't need to turn much. The hole would not be deep.

"Let me help you."

22

"No." She stabbed and scraped. "He was my dog."

She did not look but she felt Papa watch as she hacked at the frozen earth. She was on her knees, holding the shovel with both hands. She stabbed at the ground with quick angry movements.

"We could make a fire," he suggested. She looked up at him, quickly, and with horror. "To thaw the ground," he explained.

Gjerta shook her head. The fur of her hood tickled her eyes so she brushed it back and off and returned to digging.

Her father had told her once that the lights they saw in the sky, the lights from the stars, were ghosts. That by the time the light was close enough for them to see, it had already travelled for centuries and the sun it came from was already gone. She should have realised that Major was like that. She should have known, as soon as she took the puppy from her father's hands, that the animal was already on its way to dying. There were darkteeth in the woods. They lived amongst the trees and in the shadows between them and where else was a puppy going to play?

"It's not your fault."

Her tears were too cold to fall. It meant her eyes were full of stars. They fractured her vision into shining multiples; she saw a thousand clods of soil and tossed snow, and when she looked at where Major lay, wrapped in cloth, she saw more of him. Saw him everywhere, lots of dogs, all dead.

"It's not your fault," her father said again. When he put a hand upon her shoulder and made to kneel beside her, she said, "I know, Papa," hoping it would stop him. But it didn't, and he knelt and held her, thick with fur and wild curled hair.

The pair of them must have looked like pagans, knelt before an evergreen tree in worship. It was not the first time they had done so. This was Mama's tree.

"I wish we had buried your mother here."

"She's here anyway," Gjerta said, though she wished it too. Mama was buried at a cemetery far away from the woods, miles away, in town. Papa had taken her there, "Because she didn't want to be here anymore." But she never wanted to be here before and it didn't make a difference to him then. He wouldn't let her go. In the end, she went anyway.

Gjerta had heard her leave in the night. She heard the door bang shut, even quietly, and she had looked out the window to see her mother's red coat disappearing into the darkness between the trees. She was looking up at them as she did at Christmas, looking for the right one, one that was perfect, and yet they still had a few weeks before it was necessary. At first, Gjerta wondered if this was how her Mama always found the right one so quickly; she'd already looked a few weeks in advance. Then Gjerta noticed she was walking awkwardly and wondered if she was sleepwalking. She was carrying a ladder, the little step ladder they kept in the cupboard, but Gjerta didn't know that then. She had called to her, "Mama," but she called quietly so as not to disturb Papa. She did not like her mother out where the darkteeth were, not at night, not when they could hide better, so she had put on her coat and her boots and gone running after her. Papa said if you were warm enough when you went out then you were wearing too many clothes, but Gjerta had only her nightie and boots.

She knew she was too late because she heard the darkteeth snapping, and though the sound was her mother's feet kicking at the ladder where it leaned against the tree, Gjerta did not see it, not then, not until she was older. All she saw was her Mama twisting in the moon-coloured snow-glow. Her father had found her there, staring. He'd said the same words then as now.

"I am sorry."

Gjerta did not know who he was saying it to.

*

"Can't sleep?"

Gjerta had been staring at the ceiling, listening for noises in the wind outside. She wondered if she had made some noise herself to have disturbed Søren. "I'm fine," she told him.

She was cold. She was as fully dressed as was sensible inside the sleeping bag and was still freezing. Her clothes were so stiff with cold it felt like she wore the winter in layers. The exertion of seeing to the dogs and then burying Voksen had warmed her, and coming inside where Søren had both the stoves going to cook dinner, her skin had prickled with heat. But that seemed long ago now. The building was small to gather body heat more effectively—as a hide for hunting there was little need for much room anyway—but now it felt like the walls had fallen and the wind was all around them, howling like heartbreak.

"Are you worried?" Søren asked.

She turned, thinking she'd catch him staring, but Søren was on his side, wrapped up tight in his sleeping bag and facing away from her. Maybe it had been her breathing that told him she was awake. "Worried?"

"About bears."

She shifted again, fidgeting in her bedding, and looked at where she had laid her blanket. It did little to disguise the shapes beneath it. Søren had warned her with a gesture of his spoon as he stirred their dinner, pointing to a heap of traps on the floor as she unwound her scarf and stamped the snow from her boots. The traps were the only things in the hide. Like the pole outside, they had been stained with dark colours, but Gjerta thought it was probably rust. She had done her best to ignore them, watching Søren prepare their meal. The ice Søren had breathed into his beard was melting. He broke the frost away from beneath his nostrils, scraped it from the hair of his moustache, and sniffed a lot as he adjusted to the new temperature. He stirred their usual mix of soup and pasta and canned meats; never enough to replace the calories they lost travelling, but hot. It would warm them from the inside. He did not care about the metal traps, shut and safe as he thought them to be.

Now the stove-fires were out and she was frigid with cold, even in her insulated sleeping bag. Melt-water dripped from the roof and walls outside, but it would quickly freeze again. The skin of Gjerta's face was tight with cold. It felt like it would crack when she spoke. "I am not worried about bears," she said, staring at the bulk beneath her blanket. "The dogs will warn us."

Gjerta was not surprised at Søren's concern. Earlier, she had opened the map across the floor to confirm where they were. The north-east of Greenland was a ragged line, with a lot of ground to cover. Nevertheless, they should have arrived back at Daneborg on the twenty-second of December. They were two days late, and still somewhere too far north, trapped between the peaks of mountains and icebergs.

"Jørgensen?" Søren had asked.

"Hmm?"

"I said do you want me to move them?"

The offer had made little sense to Gjerta; Søren could not move mountains, could not alter the path of icebergs. But Gjerta had been staring at the bear traps, not the map. She said she was fine and covered them with her blanket.

Staring at it now, shivering, she considered taking it back.

Her name came out of the darkness.

"Jørgensen?"

She said nothing. She pretended to sleep. She knew what he was going to say next and he would only be half joking.

"Jørgensen? Do you want to—"

"No."

"Okay."

"Thank you."

"I was only joking."

"I know."

She closed her eyes and tried to sleep. She couldn't. It was cold and it was never quiet here, and usually she didn't mind, but tonight the wind outside and the sounds of the ground, the creaking, groaning, moans of the land, reminded her of home. Occasionally she heard the awful hammering of an iceberg settling, the grinding of ice on ice as the wind brought it to her, and it sounded like trees falling. Other times, the wind shifted and what she heard was the Foehn wind coming off the ice sheet between the mountains. It meant a warmer temperature and perhaps less snow, which was good, but the sound it made reminded her of Major. The way he had howled in the woods. Papa had brought him back wrapped in his coat. By then the dog was dead.

"Was it the darkteeth?"

Her father had frowned, puzzled, and said no. But puzzled as he'd been, she could tell he was lying. "It was his time," was all he said. He cleaned the dog's fur before allowing her to bury him, but Gjerta still saw the bite marks.

Outside, the wind howled and screamed.

"Søren?"

"Yes? I am awake."

She didn't know how to say it. How to bring it up now that so much time had passed since he'd tried himself.

She didn't need to. It must have been in her voice, underneath her words. She heard him moving in his sleeping bag, felt him shift in the dark and come to her, and then she was enveloped. She clutched at him as he moved against her, helped him fumble with the layers of clothing when she was warm, and then she clutched him within a warmth of her own, and she rolled so he lay beneath her and she held him close and smelt the musk of the furs he had worn on his skin and she held his bearded face to her breasts and eventually he called her Gjerta and she cried out like a shriek of Arctic wind, sharp and sudden and then gone.

Afterwards, he tried to cover her with the blanket she'd discarded. "Leave it," she told him. He gave her his own blanket instead and they slept.

*

"It is the brightest star in the heavens. I keep telling you this, Gjerta."

"Because it's a dream, Papa."

Gjerta was an adult version of the girl her Papa was talking to, but it did not matter. They were looking at the star on their Christmas tree but it was not outside their cabin. It was outside the poacher's lodge, which they visited more and more often.

"The stars watch over you. And guide you."

"Like Mama," said Gjerta, because she saw her hanging in the Christmas tree. The rope had slipped down the branch towards the trunk and she was kicking at where the ladder would have been if it was her tree, the one she had chosen. Each kick turned her body, but wherever she went she looked down into her daughter's eyes.

"Sirius is part of Canis Major. It guards the heavens, keeps them safe."

"Yes Papa." She was looking at her mother looking at her.

"It guards the heavens," Papa said, looking up into the branches of the tree, "And keeps out those who have no business being there."

Gjerta's mother was kicking at dogs that jumped for her feet. Every time their jaws snapped closed came the sound of a kicked stepladder.

"This isn't the right tree," said Gjerta.

"None of this is right," said her Papa.

Gjerta crouched and called the dogs to her. One by one they ran to her and died in her arms. She put them on the ground and they sank into the snow at the base of the tree.

"Let me help you," her Papa said.

"No," said Gjerta. "They were my dogs."

But the dog she held now was not a dog.

"It's not your fault."

What she held now was something she did not want to see. It was bright and glistening and small and cold and it shone and it looked like her. She put it on the ground and stood, raising the rifle.

"You'll carry her with you forever," said Papa. He touched his chest, his heart, like he did when he talked about Mama.

"And you," said Gjerta.

"And me."

"And all of the trees."

Above them, a woman kicked at the bark of her tree and each time she struck it came the sound of a rifle shot.

"She always found the perfect tree like this," said Papa. When he snapped his fingers it echoed around the forest and a thousand traps sprang up out of the snow, snapping their metal teeth on the wind.

*

"Glaedelig Jul," Søren said.

Gjerta rubbed sleep from her face because she couldn't smile. "Yes," she said. "Merry Christmas."

On one stove, Søren was stirring their breakfast. From the other he removed a pan and tipped it to a cup. "We had a visitor last night." He handed Gjerta coffee as she sat up in her sleeping bag. "The dogs were agitated."

She took the cup in both hands and sipped at it, hot as it was. "Santa Claus," she said, but she imagined a man in furs with a sack full of traps.

Søren smiled. "Nisse maybe."

Nisse, mischievous elf that played pranks on people around Christmas. You were supposed to leave him some food on Christmas Eve to avoid the worst ones, but Gjerta never had. Perhaps she should have.

Søren tipped the breakfast pan to metal bowls and sprinkled something over both. When he handed the food to her, Gjerta was surprised to find rice pudding with a lacing of cinnamon. Risengrød. She hadn't had it for years.

Søren spooned the food to his mouth, wiping creamy sauce from his beard with the back of his hand. "There's aebleskiver, too."

"Really?"

Mama used to make the aebleskiver cakes. After she died, Papa had never tried.

"No," Søren said, worried his joke had been mean. "Sorry."

They ate quietly. Outside the wind cut against the corners of their cabin. It was the only sound. Whatever had disturbed the dogs in the night was not bothering them now.

"Last night—"

"Can you turn the stoves off," Gjerta asked.

"Too hot?"

Søren was joking again but Gjerta nodded. Eating her grød, she didn't see him reach for her until his hand was on her face. She pulled back suddenly. "Don't."

"Sorry."

"Sorry," she said as well. "Sorry."

"You have a temperature." He reached out again. He moved slowly, as if she might snap at him again. As if she might bite. He put his palm to her cheek and the coolness of his skin told her the truth of his words. He touched her forehead too, and then her cheek again. "You are not well."

His thumb rubbed gently at her cheekbone and Gjerta worried she might be crying. That he was wiping away a tear. When he said, "How did you get this?" she realised it was the scar she could not see, the one beneath her eye.

She put her bowl down and stood up from her insulated sleeping bag. "I want to check the dogs."

Søren said nothing. He tipped her grød back into the pan as she dressed. "Take the rifle," he said, but she had it already, stepping out into the cold.

Outside, the first thing Gjerta saw was the foil star upon the replaced bait pole and she wondered if Søren had lied about the night-noises so she would come out and check. She did not smile. As she passed, she plucked the star from the pole and cast it to a wind that was no longer there. The morning was suddenly still and quiet and the star lay in the snow, barely fluttering.

She checked for the tracks of a polar bear visit. She found only their own, animal prints and sled runners like evidence of Santa Claus. Nothing near the cabin of course, or the dogs would have been more than agitated. If there had been a polar bear it clearly wasn't hungry yet. But they were known to stalk patrols. Some even killed their own cubs if they needed to.

She checked behind, making sure the building was still in sight. Habits of caution were good habits to cultivate, so she checked even though the weather was fine. Visibility was good, but the cabin had been painted white so that even where it wasn't covered in snow, even in fine weather, it was difficult to see. She was struck by the effort of it all; who would build and paint such a place out here? Only the light from its single window told her it was there and that was dimmed, a cataract of paper taped to the frame inside. It reminded her of a joke her father had told her about an Arctic fox giving advice to a polar bear. The bear had asked the fox how it knew it was being hunted. Do you hear me in the wind, it had asked. Surely you cannot see me upon the snow. And the fox had pointed to the bear's black nose. Gjerta didn't like how the joke ended, poor fox, and the memory did nothing to make her smile either.

She looked around in the snow for signs. The ground was pristine except where she'd trodden it. If there was a bear out here, it was hiding its nose. If there had been one in the night, it had hidden its tracks.

Gjerta had once emerged from the tent she shared with Søren to see the lumbering hulk of a polar bear passing, its fur a dirty yellow and its muzzle brown with dried blood where its tongue couldn't reach. It had looked at her and shown its teeth in a protracted yawn before continuing on its way. None of the dogs had stirred, not even Poncho. Perhaps they had been visited by the same bear, an Arctic ghost passing them in the night.

She went to the dogs. "Did we have a visitor last night?" she asked them. She threw the question to each one with their breakfast. "Did someone come last night?"

Each dog offered her some sort of answer. Each dog except one. Her favourite, the eldest, lay dead in the snow. A solid shape of frozen fur.

*

After her mother died, Gjerta didn't play much. It was something her father was not very good at. He was good at teaching her things. To compensate, he bought her a puppy. He had travelled into town, something he did as rarely as possible, and returned with a Husky. "Good in the cold," he explained. Gjerta called it Major after Canis Major, the constellation that held the power of the dog star, brightest in the night sky. Sirius.

Papa approved. "The dog star guards the heavens," he said. "Keeps them safe." He was rough with the fur around Major's neck, and swatted him up under the muzzle with affection he wasn't used to giving. "He'll watch over you."

"Like Mama?"

"Yes, like Mama. She's up there, too. Amongst the stars."

"Where?"

Gjerta had looked, holding her new puppy up so he could see.

"Far away. Too far away to see. Like the lines of the constellations. But she's there. The stars are the light of heaven, shining through holes in the dark."

"Papa..."

But she couldn't finish.

"You can ask."

"Is Mama a ghost?"

It wasn't the question he had been expecting. Even as a child, Gjerta recognised the surprise. She recognised the relief, too.

"Do you think she's a ghost?" he asked.

"I see her sometimes. Between the trees."

Sometimes she saw her in the shadows of her room, or reflected in the glass of her window. A couple of times she thought she lay beneath the lodge, within the crawl space of its trapdoor. She did not mention this.

"Sometimes I hear her, Papa."

"Maybe you do. Sometimes I see her too. But it doesn't mean she's there. It means she's here." He placed his hand on his chest, over his heart, and then he put it over hers. "She's in you." He caressed her face, tucked a strand of hair behind her ear.

And then he explained about the stars and their ghost-light, that they both saw her although she wasn't really there, and Gjerta didn't ask anything else, even though she wanted to.

*

Looking up at the sky now, Gjerta saw it turn colour. It had lightened with a day that never fully came and dancing across it were hues of green. Waves that moved fast and were gone, replaced again by others. The aurora borealis. Charged particles from the sun, reacting with the atoms and ions in the atmosphere. Her father had not told her this; she learned this later. Her father had told her the lights came from the Valkyries, the light reflecting from their shields as they carried the dead from the battlefield.

"They are always beautiful," Søren said, emerging from inside.

"The Valkyries," Gjerta said. She explained what her father had told her without mentioning him.

"Perhaps it is them," Søren admitted. "There is always a war somewhere."

Gjerta agreed.

"I was told the light was Freja, riding her horse across the sky, cloak billowing behind," Søren said. "The light is the magic of her passing."

Gjerta nodded. "Odin's wife, and his daughter as well," she said. "She knew the future, but she could not change it."

"That's Frigg. Freja is the fertility goddess and she rules over the afterlife. Those who do not go with the Valkyries go to her."

Yes, Gjerta thought. She lives between the stars.

"Sometimes she weeps for her absent husband. When that happens the lights are not green but red."

They watched the sky together, waves of a silent sea washing across it. The ground caught its glow. Tinged green, the two of them stood not upon snow but a vast forest floor. They stood in a wood without trees, a land as green as its name promised.

"The dead are calling," said Gjerta.

Søren nodded. "The people here believe the light is the afterlife itself, a place of fair weather, good hunting, and play. Some say it is only the babies that play, the children..." He shrugged. "I like it."

He nodded again, this time to the sky, and set to readying the sled.

Gjerta looked to where she'd heaped snow over Voksen, a mound by the side of the hut.

"Valkyrie," she said.

Søren turned, expecting more talk of the sky.

"Our Valkyrie. She's dead."

Søren shook his head. He stamped at the snow and looked at her again. "Show me."

The dog was frosted with snow, fur stiff with ice. Søren knelt and rubbed at the body but stopped when he felt how hard it had become. "Can't run forever," he said to it. To Gjerta he said, "Exhaustion?"

"I want to bury her."

"I can do it." He stood and went to the sled.

Gjerta stared at the dog. When Søren returned with the shovel, she took it from him. She'd had more practice burying things. "You can do it next time, maybe."

*

The first time Gjerta heard her father leave the cabin late one Christmas Eve, she had panicked. She went to the window in such a rush that she hit her head against it. She saw him step into the darkness between the trees, yelled for him, "Papa!" but he disappeared behind the cloud her breath made on the glass without turning back. As before, with Mama, she pulled her boots on and ran out into the cold but he was already gone, swallowed up by the forest. She chased after him, worried she knew where he was going. Not the lodge, not without her, but the tree.

Gjerta had forgotten where the tree was, and her father would not tell her. It was a secret he kept from her, even when she explained how worried she was that one day they might pick it out for Christmas. He told her they would never cut it down, but she still worried.

When she found him, and the tree, she wondered how she had ever forgotten it.

"Papa."

He let her stay with him, but she could tell he didn't want her there. He did not say so—he said it was good that she had come—but she could hear the thoughts beneath his words and in the years that followed she did not go with him when she heard him leave on a Christmas Eve. She waited, kneeling at the edge of the bed so she could see him return, but she did not go with him.

One year, when she was older, she watched him stomp his way through the snow, heard its crunch beneath his feet, and she waited for the woods to swallow him. She was left with only her reflection in the glass, peering in from the dark. It didn't seem like hers. She told it, "Goodbye."

When she stood up from the covers of her bed, she was already dressed. Her backpack was stuffed full with clothes and she had written her father a letter. She put it with his Christmas gift and tried to leave but when she looked up from the snow she trod upon she found herself at the tree and was not surprised.

Papa was staring into its height.

"How long to choose this one?" he asked. He did not turn around to greet Gjerta. Who else would it be in the dark forest with him if not her? Who else could it be?

"Not long," Gjerta said, but only because he expected her to. She thought perhaps with this one Mama took her time. Choosing the tree was the only freedom she ever really had.

Her father nodded, still looking up into the branches. Gjerta suspected he nodded at her thoughts rather than her words.

"I am haunted by this tree," he said.

Gjerta understood.

"I left you a note," she said.

He did not reply. He did not move. He stared into the branches as if Mama was still there. She wondered if he saw her kicking or if she was still. Gjerta would always remember her kicking.

"Papa? I left it with your present."

Still he did not move or speak. Gjerta wondered if he wanted her to leave him. She wondered why she had not already.

"It's a compass," she said. "Your present. So you can find the way when the stars are gone."

"Look," he said. He gestured with his hand, come here, come here, without turning to face her, and though she did not want to, Gjerta went to him. "Look," he said again, and switched on his torch.

Above them, the night frost glistened like the stars of Christmas lights, the underside of each branch aglitter with ice. The snow-laden leaves sparkled as he tossed quick arcs of light across them, dazzling her with a display that was beautiful and morbid at once. She knew the word morbid now.

"Papa," she said.

But he had found it. The light settled on one particular branch where the bark had been stripped away. He traced the length of it, aiming his light along the slope the rope had stuttered down under Mama's swinging weight. Gjerta did not like the way he looked at it.

"It never heals," he said.

Gjerta put her arm around him and he lowered the beam.

"Why did she do it?" he asked. It was the question he'd expected her to ask long ago.

But Gjerta was looking at where her father's light now rested. It cut a low angle down to the ground and she could see where three names had been carved. Her mother's name. Cut into the bark below: Major. And finally, close to the ground: Stella. Gjerta had not carved the names. She did not want the darkteeth to find them again.

She turned from him, from all of them, and she ran.

Her father called after her, "Gjerta!" but he did not follow. In the years that came after, she wondered if she wanted him to.

*

Gjerta and Søren hushed their way across a frozen sea of grey without horizon. The aurora had been brief, and now the pearl sky was again the gloom of night. The sled bumped violently where the snow was thin, the rock and ice beneath exposed by a Foehn wind that swept the snow away and warmed what was left. Gjerta listened for a voice within it but heard nothing. She listened for the snapping of teeth but did not hear that either, though she knew it was there. They rushed deeper into the Arctic, the remaining dogs churning the snow, the runners of the Morten Pine and their skis leaving long lines behind them. She thought of the dogs buried behind them on that trail, left like offerings not to Nisse but to the darkteeth.

Søren windmilled his arms. Gjerta did too, though she was too warm. When she changed arms she allowed the sled to get away from her for a moment, just a moment, so that when she took hold again she was slightly behind Søren. Beyond his peripheral vision. She waited for the snow. Not a whiteout, nothing heavy enough for caution; just enough to provide some cover.

Daneborg was close now. They were three dogs down, but they were lighter, much lighter, and they were faster. The dogs did not tire so quickly. They would reach Daneborg today, Søren and the dogs.

Gjerta would not. When the wind brought the snow, as she knew it would, she let go of the sled and dropped back, dropped behind, watching as the blinking lights of it sped away from her. She thought of Odin the father god on his eight-legged horse Sleipnir, thundering across the sky in eternal hunt. She thought of how any companion giving up was turned to dust and gone and she held her arms out to slow her momentum. She was a star on the snow, slowing...slowing...

Still.

As soon as she had stopped, she turned around, lifting her skis carefully and setting them down again into the slush of her own tracks. She began to ski back the way they had come, quick but steady, following her own parallels. She did not know how long she had before Søren noticed. The hush of her skis was buried beneath the sound of the Foehn. You do not hear me in the wind, she thought. She switched off her headlamp. You do not see me upon the snow.

She made her way back.

*

Gjerta often thought about going back home. She imagined her Papa's joy, and wondered if he would be proud of her—she was Siriuspatruljen—but thought perhaps he would be upset instead; everything he had taught her she had taken elsewhere. Not knowing how he would react was one of the reasons she did not return. Not knowing how she would react was another. Would she go back to the lodge, or would she open it up with her father's axe, open it up so the dark could come out? What would live there in its place? No animals ever had, even when the door had been open.

She thought of all her father had taught her—not because he was a cruel man, but because he wanted her unafraid—and she thought about the woman she was able to give him in return and she wondered if the trade had been fair.

"Do you think she's a ghost? Do you think she sees?"

She no longer remembered who asked, perhaps they both did, but Gjerta thought she knew the answer. She thought her Papa knew as well and it made her regret leaving so quickly that night at the tree. She should have cut it down first so her Papa could do nothing foolish while she was away. There were a thousand

thousand other trees he could choose but Gjerta did not care as long as he could not have that one.

When she imagined it, she offered him the axe for the final swings and this time he took it from her. He would bring the axe up and around and down, again and again, until the tree fell and the crackling of its cold timber would sound like a thousand thousand traps snapping closed, all at once.

*

She saw the star, guiding her in on its bait pole, and she did not care who had put it there, only hoped that it was real. All the way back she had seen faces beneath the snow, rising up from the ground like masks of frost as she rushed past them on skis that told them shh. Sometimes they were her face, sometimes his. Now they were gone, and all that rose up were the mounds of the snow she had made as graves.

She unclipped her skis at the door of the hide, dropping each one outside. She did not know how much time she had.

As if to hurry her, green aurora light danced across the sky, quick as the flash it was. A tossed ribbon of colour that told her hurry, hurry, the stars are gone. Hurry, or you will be lost with them.

She set the rifle down on the floor and shrugged off her pack, letting it fall behind her, and went straight to the traps. She dragged them outside.

The snow was falling sideways, carried by a fierce wind that screamed with her own voice. Buried inside it, she heard a child cry.

She dragged the traps in a tumble of metal jaws and chain, past the bait pole, and pinned them open in the snow. She buried them like she had her dogs. Like she had buried everything else. She surrounded herself with deadly secrets in the snow, each one a silent scream choked full of the snow that hid it, each one waiting to snap shut on the wind. She would know when they did. She always heard them.

She had left the rifle inside. When she turned back for the building it was lost to her and all she saw was white. But there! She had left the door open, kept it that way with her pack, and she saw a slice of darkness deeper than the night and starless. She headed for it.

She would not stay. She retrieved the rifle and headed back to where the darkteeth waited.

The ground behind her was cracking, she could feel it. She did not hear it, but she felt the ice she walked on crack and break and flood with dark rising water that would clutch her and drown her, fill her mouth with its own, and freeze her from the inside. She hurried, panting as she ran, legs held by snow that wanted her still. Then, as sudden as if she had fallen through into the cold Arctic sea, she was inside the circle she had made, a circle of circles ready to bite, and she slumped into the snow against the bait pole. She had no flesh to offer but her own. It was all she had ever had.

I know you are coming.

She yanked off her scarf and shoved her hood down. She was hot. Her skin tightened with a new cold. The wind took her scarf, and it took her hat when she cast it aside. She swept her mask up from her face to keep her hair back. It knocked her lamp off but that was fine. She turned it off and pushed it into the snow.

You do not see me...

She took up the rifle, and she watched, and she waited.

Gjerta had thought she would find peace in this treeless place, but like the first settlers who had come thinking the land was green, all she found was somewhere barren, shaped by glacial pressure. The slow movements of heavy ice had scraped scars that ran deep and pressed so hard that the ground bowed beneath it, waiting for it to leave so it could form a shape of its own. But it would never leave, not completely. There was always ice, and always snow, and forever there would be the wind and the things within it.

A violent gust finally took the star from the pole and it flashed away as if carried by the aurora, taken by whatever or whoever turned the sky above into wonderful waves of green light. She thought of her own star, named only so her father would have something to carve.

"Stella."

Gjerta took off her gloves to trace the name in the bark beside her, thinking nothing of the sudden tree where the bait pole used to be. She traced the lines of her own name, too. Papa must have carved it there after she left.

I am haunted by this tree, she thought. By all of them. And I always will be.

The tree was tall and lit with lights she'd made for Christmas, but hanging from its branches, amongst the decorations, her mother looked down at her with a face more her own than she remembered. Despite how much her father told her so.

She tucked the rifle between her knees to hold it and rubbed at her face with both hands. She was hot, but that did not matter.

When she took her hands away again, the tree was gone. Her mother was gone.

She would not be far, though. Even now, Gjerta heard her voice in the snow, the whispering hiss of it, the here and gone of it. She had buried the radio, but the voice she'd heard in the crackle of its static was all around her and there was winter in it. She strained to hear the words but all she heard were her own.

"I am sorry," she said. "I am sorry."

She said it because it was true, and now the man of traps could come. She would let him. The star on the pole was gone, the stars above too, but Gjerta would be the one to guide him. He would need no compass, no constellations but her. Her light was bright, burning her up from inside. She shone with it.

White amongst the white, a hulking shape lumbered near. It came to her, turning a path this way and that, avoiding her traps of darkteeth and yawning its own at her. It was a polar bear, mouth suddenly clutching its own cub, a dog, a dead human baby that dropped from its teeth and was nothing, pulled apart into snow and scattered by the wind before it could reach a ground too frozen to bury it.

The bear dispersed into the same snow that had formed it. Heading to her through its fading shape was -

"Papa!"

She called to him though he was far away.

The man that came was a mass of fur and clothing, a trapper dressed in the skins of his kills, and rattling around him on lengths of chain were the teeth of his traps and the teeth of hers. He wore them as armour, as she did. He dragged them wherever he went and as he came they snapped closed on the air behind him. They turned and tumbled and opened and closed as they followed his course towards her. He called names under the sound of the wind. The wind was his breath and his voice was the clapping, snapping, trapping sound of darkteeth.

To herald his coming, the aurora turned from green to red. It cast wounds across the sky that made the snow bleed.

Gjerta checked the rifle was loaded. The cold of its metal stuck at her skin.

When she was young, Gjerta didn't understand how a trapper's lodge could also be a poacher's lodge. There had been frames outside for all to see, yet a secret place inside. As she grew up, she understood it better.

She hefted the rifle up into her armpit.

The man in the snow, dragging his traps, calling names, wore the skin of her father. It sagged around him, loose on a frame too slight to fill it, but she thought she heard something of his voice when he called to her.

"Papa?"

She tried again to hear the name he'd used—Gjerta? Jørgensen? —and raised the rifle ready to fire. She would fire until the man fell, until the barking sounds of the darkteeth stopped snapping and were finally shut.

BONUS MATERIAL

There's a well known saying that claims "a picture paints a thousand words". Some people think this means a picture is better than a thousand words, but if pictures were better we'd have one instead of a saying, wouldn't we? Anyway, it's a good idea to play around with, especially if you change the verb to "suggests"...

Here's a piece of "flash" fiction, camera pun fully intended. And yeah, I used a thousand words.

IT'S BEGINNING TO LOOK A LOT LIKE...

Picture this: There's a young couple standing near the low railings of Westminster Bridge. Big Ben and The Houses of Parliament stretch behind them at the river side. It's snowing lightly. The man is reaching towards the edge of the shot, your left, because he's taking the picture himself, and the woman is pulling strands of long wind-blown hair from her face. She's pretty. So is he. The kind of couple relatives are unreasonably proud of as they predict the beauty of future children. She wears an "I HEART LONDON" jumper and he wears a Union Flag badge on his jacket. Tourists. Both of them are smiling. Big Ben stands proud beside them, but it's just a clock next to their happy faces.

Picture this: The giant Christmas tree of Trafalgar Square, the couple far enough away that it fits almost entirely in the shot with them. Again the man holds the camera for their photo. The young woman points behind her, grinning, and though a lot of the snow on the leaves may be fake her festive cheer is not, and nor are the flakes on her coat and in her hair. The man has a dusting of them in his eyelashes. People behind look at the tree in small groups or are passing and ignore it on their way elsewhere.

Picture this: A shopping street of decorated archways, the lights bright white but in sharp focus. It must be a good camera. There's a large Debenhams and the woman presents it with both arms like a hostess on a game show. The man is not in this picture, but you can somehow sense him smiling from where you are, looking at her. She's grinning, perhaps more than she had for the Christmas tree, and in the next shot you're expecting to see shopping bags.

Video footage. The battery light is flashing as the camera fills with the image of someone's boots, then lifts to show the couple are posing together in front of a choir in the street, or rather in front of a crowd gathering around the choir in the street. Voices sing something traditional, angelic in harmony but losing the words to an unseen band somewhere. Both of them have their hands full with, yep, those expected shopping bags; someone else holds the camera for them. They are smiling frozen smiles, waiting for the picture, then break from their pose as they realise what has happened. The man reaches for the camera, his words foreign but polite. The woman mimes switching a button. Tourists. There's a blur of motion—sleeves and pockets and legs, a pavement flashing back and forth—as whoever holds the camera runs. Eventually the disorientating motion stops and the camera is raised to show the young man looking around a crowded street. He looks angry. Eventually the woman appears, carrying all the shopping but still managing to clutch at his arm, looking around with him as someone chuckles softly. It makes the camera shake.

Picture this: They're at the foot of the London Eye, near the front of the queue. It's lit up. They're looking to its top and the height makes them seem small. They don't know to pose for the photo. Whoever takes it does so from far away.

Picture this: They stand before the fence of Buckingham Palace. She has put her shopping down and is holding the black bars, looking beyond the golden spikes at the grand building behind. Her companion is looking to the right at one of the red-clad fur-topped guards. The guard looks forward, ignoring them both.

Picture this: The couple are walking one of London's busy streets. Some of the snow here has been trodden brown. They're both looking down at it as they walk. Their bags look heavy. The picture has been taken from behind.

Picture this: They enter a hotel.

Picture this: The couple are sleeping. Their room is clean, simple. A scattering of coins on the bedside table next to a London map and an alarm clock. A teddy bear dressed in a blue overcoat, wearing a black hat, stands over it all. In the bed, the man is a covered shape behind the woman, spooning her body with his. The flash has not woken them.

Picture this: The couple are on top of the bedclothes. They're awake now. Bound. Bloody faced. The man is tied front down on the bed, eyes wide, muscle taut as he strains towards the girl beside him. The woman has been tied face up, looking at her lover, terrified. He wears a pair of white boxer shorts, she wears a t-shirt far too big for her. Both have black tape over their mouths. The bedside table has been knocked away but still stands. It now holds a tangle of leftover cord and the roll of tape. The bear has landed upright leaning into the corner as if it can't stand to see.

Video footage. The battery light is flashing. Both are screaming behind the tape on their mouths, but the sounds are only muffled Ms. A man steps into shot, approaching the girl. He wears a blue boiler suit with a reindeer mask and a Santa hat instead of antlers. The camera moves for a better angle when he blocks the shot of the couple on the bed. He turns then, gestures for the person with the camera to put it down. A cluttered night table is wiped clear of perfumes and makeup items and the camera rocks and jostles into a new position where they used to be. Another man in a boiler suit, masked as a coal-eyed snowman with a long carrot nose and incongruous reindeer antlers, approaches the bed on the bound male side. The two Christmas figures face each other, standing big as Ben, and play a round of paper stone scissors. The man on the left plays stone. The man on the right, scissors.

The battery dies.

THE RAIN DEER

Dasher, Dancer, Prancer…

Leah recited the names silently as she raced around the dark country lanes, her eyes on the road and her foot heavy on the accelerator. She wasn't so much dashing through the snow as speeding through the sleet, the narrow verges either side blurred smudges of dark slush, the road shining wet. She knew the roads well, and she knew the dangers, and so she knew she was travelling way too fast. She kept her foot down anyway. There was satisfaction to be had in each hard corner, the swish of mud and slush under the tyres. The wipers were squeaking back and forth and she used them to mark a rhythm in her head.

…Vix-en, Com-et, Cu-pid…

She hated Christmas, fucking hated it, though she tried not to. This year she'd bought everything he said, had prepped the turkey and forgone the "cranberry shit", bought beers instead of wine, put up a fake tree instead of a real one, even though it was her who cleaned up "the crap" that fell from a dying pine. And still they couldn't make it through the holiday without arguing. Christmas Eve, and here she was careening her way around the countryside when she should have been at home with her husband and daughter.

…Donner, Blitzen…

Thunder and lightning.

Leah hadn't named the reindeer for years. It had been a tactic of her mother's. "Name the reindeer, honey," she'd say, and Leah would close her eyes to think and cover her ears to block out the sound of Mum and Dad arguing, mouthing the names silently so as not to disturb them as they cried and shouted.

Dasher, Dancer, Prancer, Vixen, Comet, Cupid, Donner, Blitzen. And then again from the beginning: Dasher, Dancer, Prancer...

She took a corner so tight that the car rocked and she was thrown sideways into the door before taking a sharp dig in the hips from the gear stick. The wheels threw up muddy puddles and old snow before finding grip again. This was what she did now instead of naming reindeer: she drove.

The rain was falling in silver sheets, diagonal lines held in the beams of the headlights. Leah cranked the window down so the cold and wet could keep her alert, could keep her mind off of what had happened at home. She used some of the rain water to wipe crusts of blood from her nostrils.

Ahead, in the rain-lashed dark, Leah glimpsed a movement. It bounded in from the right, quick, springing out of the trees, too fast for her to see until it stopped and even then she had difficulty because of how it shimmered. A shape of rain more dense than that which fell around it, a silvered deer swelling in size as the rain gave it substance. It glistened wet with what had made it, diagonal lines blurring and brightening in the headlights. It stared at her with empty sockets, cavities of night where no rain sparkled.

Leah slammed both feet to the brake pedal but the wheels locked and she aquaplaned. She struck the deer but all it did was burst into a spray that washed up the bonnet and windscreen, only to be tossed aside by the wipers as she passed through.

When her view cleared, she found the rain had stopped. The change was as sudden as the impact had been; it was simply no longer raining.

Ahead, a parked car was flashing hazard lights.

"Dammit!"

Leah resisted the urge to wrench the wheel, knowing it would put her into the trees. Instead, she pumped at the brakes again, coming to a halt abrupt enough to test the strength of her seatbelt. She felt her nose run and wiped at it with her sleeve. It was bleeding again.

"Fucking Rudolph," she said to the rear view mirror, cleaning herself. She sat panting through her mouth in time with the flashing amber lights of the parked vehicle.

It looked abandoned.

Leah put on her own hazard lights but did not leave the car. She moved it slowly forward, looking inside the other one as she passed. There was no one, just an open box on the passenger seat. She looked beyond the car but saw only a fallen fence and the dark between the trees. She checked the other side.

A body hung from a tree. It twitched and jerked.

Leah pulled herself out of the car and into the cold. The body lurched and twisted as she approached and she saw that it wasn't what she had supposed: it was a deer. It had been strung up by its hind legs. The snow below was dark with blood. The smell was overpowering, rich and pungent with the odour of offal and excrement, all of which had been trodden into the ground around it.

Leah retched, bending to vomit, and saw hot tangles of entrails steaming in the cool night air. A pair of boots stepped into them and she flinched upright again as a man emerged from behind the carcass. He held a knife in one bloody fist.

Leah didn't scream but a hushed exhalation clouded the air between them.

The man raised his other hand to her, the one without the knife.

He showed her his palm and spread fingers. "Sorry!" he said, "Sorry."

Leah took a single step back, but that was all. The deer, no longer tugged by the actions of the man's blade, only twisted on its rope. Its stomach had been opened up. Much of it had been scraped out, a chunky puddle staining the ground. Its throat gaped open and the limp head was bloody with what had drained from it. Under the tree, the rain had done little to wash it clean.

"It's okay," said the man. "If you're not the one who killed it, it's okay. The law says so."

Leah realised this man was carving up road kill.

"You didn't hit it," she said.

"No."

Leah knew a lie when a man told one.

"It was an accident?"

"Yeah," he said. "An accident."

Leah looked at the hollowed body.

"Can you do me next?" she said.

The man, wiping his hands on a rag, stopped to say, "What?"

Leah shook her head.

"Look, Miss, you won't tell anyone will you?"

But she was already leaving him. Slow. Calm. Back in the car she spared him a final glance. In his blood-stained coat, with a sack of something wet at his feet, he looked like some ghastly Father Christmas, but Leah could only stare into the ragged darkness of the deer's opened body. She wanted to climb inside and pull the skin closed around her.

"Merry Christmas," the man said.

The rain came again as soon as Leah started the engine and she drove away into it without looking back. She would look ahead, and keep her eyes open for more deer - they were more common around here than people thought, and accidents happened - but it was hard to watch for them with her eyes full of tears.

When she did see them, they were running ahead of the car. Eight of them, shining with a ghost light of their own. Each was a shifting shape of rain that never diminished, a silvery shimmer in the headlights. She couldn't tell if they were running from her as she drove, or taking her with them into the night, and all the while she was driving away from what she knew, she didn't care.

MISTLETOE WINE

Tina lay on her bed, looking up at the mistletoe on the ceiling. When it became blurry she realised she was crying again. She rubbed the tears away with fists, quick and hard, "For fuck's sake," and turned onto her side. But that was no good either because there, next to the clock, grinning his stupid cute grin, was Jake in that stupid lovely photograph. She slammed the picture face down with a sigh that became a growl and turned onto her back again. Better the mistletoe with its beady white eyes staring back at her than the memory of a happier time.

On the radio, Cliff Richard sang of carollers singing and new beginnings. Tina tried to ignore him. Bachelor boy Cliff wouldn't understand anyway.

"Honey, you okay in there?"

Tina sniffed so her voice wouldn't be all mucusy and said, "I'm fine, Mum." She wiped her eyes in case she came in anyway.

"He's not worth it, you know."

Tina said nothing because it was easier and after a moment she heard her mother walking away.

She looked around at her room at all the things that usually comforted her but only saw the posters of films they both liked, the CDs they'd listened to together. She even still had his jumper draped over her chair. She sat up, snatched it close, and lay back down again with it pressed to her face. She took a deep breath of him then made a pillow of it, not sure if it made her feel better or worse.

Above her, dangling from twists of sticky tape and pressed into bulbs of Blu-tack, a multitude of mistletoe berries nestled like ghostly stars amongst waxy leaves and a tangle of limp stems. A small fortune of it, dying. She tried to tell herself it had been worth it. It had felt like it at the time, and it had certainly worked, the two of them laying together beneath it all doing more than kissing. He hadn't stayed over, but he stayed long enough to show her what real love was.

One of the sprigs of mistletoe dropped. Tina flinched but otherwise didn't move. She left it where it lay, one of many scattered on the quilt she'd nestled under. She wondered if she'd be able to get up by the time her shift started. She couldn't keep calling in sick.

Tina worked in a supermarket part-time because, you know, every little helps and uni wasn't going to pay for itself. She was glad she worked there because that was where she'd met Jake. Technically he was her supervisor, technically, but really he wasn't much older than her.

He'd been so charming.

"You're working on the Christmas stand today," he'd told her.

"Christmas stand?"

They'd set up a booth in store, selling various Christmas items and offering tasters of tiny mince pies and non-alcoholic mulled wine. One of the things they were selling was mistletoe. The real stuff.

"Probably shouldn't put it next to the mince pies then," Tina had said.

"Why not?"

"It's poisonous."

"They're an aphrodisiac," he'd said.

Tina shrugged and took her position at the counter. As she straightened the Santa hat provided, Jake raised a sprig of the mistletoe above her head. "Got to make sure it works," he said. "Can't have customers complaining."

So she kissed him. Lightly, quickly, and with a blush.

Things kind of developed from there. Snowballed, if you want to be all Christmassy about it.

Tina tried not to think about that now, alone, wiping her tears with the sleeve of his discarded jumper. No, not discarded. Just forgotten. Temporarily. He'd be back for it. If he hadn't replaced it with a new one already.

Tina snorted more tears and rolled over so that only the bed heard her yell of grief. Quilt and pillow swallowed it up.

Another sprig of mistletoe fell.

Eventually, staring at nothing, Tina fell into a kind of half sleep, experiencing something that was part memory, part dream, and entirely nightmare. The club, the music, the crowd from work, all exactly as it had been at the weekend. And Jake, sitting in the chair, that girl in his lap adjusting his Santa hat, whispering in his ear, probably promising she'd be a good girl. Or maybe not, maybe the opposite. Yeah, definitely, she'd be on Santa's naughty list, that sleazy Miss Christmas with her short red skirt and skimpy top, white fur trim. Knee high boots. FMBs, the boys called them. And a sprig of mistletoe tucked into her cleavage. A mistletoe ho. Mistle-ho. Ho, ho, ho. Jake lowered his head to the mistletoe and mouthed the words, "Got to see if it works," but what Tina heard, even over the pumping music, was, "It's an aphrodisiac." As if he had no choice. "It's poison," she said, and Cliff Richard came on, Cliff Richard, singing over a heart-thumping dance beat about new beginnings and mistletoe and wine and Tina woke up to hear him still singing about it. The beat was gone, but the lyrics picked up exactly from where they'd left off in her dream-dented memory.

The mistletoe was falling from the ceiling quite regularly now, slowly burying her, as if the tape and Blu-Tack holding it there were dying too. She rolled onto her back and felt bunches of it beneath her, squashing it as more fell from the sky. She opened her mouth but caught nothing.

A time for giving, a time for getting, Cliff said. Or did he say forgiving, forgetting? She couldn't tell, though she'd heard it a million times at work. She'd never forgive or forget, but maybe she could get him back.

Give him something: get him back.

*

She stood outside his house for ten minutes, trying to ring the bell. It was snowing and she was very cold. But hearing a woman inside laugh made Tina even colder so she pressed the doorbell and waited.

She had some wine for him. A Christmas present, as if letting bygones be bygones. New Year, new start. New beginnings, eh Cliff?

Handling the mistletoe berries, she'd been reminded of frogspawn, translucent eggs with those little pips of black inside. But crushing them, the glutinous juice reminded her of semen and she thought that was appropriate. She'd scooped it up with a thick leaf and scraped it into the neck of each wine bottle. One red, one white, just to be sure.

In the wild, mistletoe was a slow killer. Spread from tree to tree by birds, it attached itself to the bark and spread its fine strands, like little ghost worms, into the tree's water. It clung on for its own life, a parasite, forever green with what it took from others. Eventually it would take everything, leaving a dry corpse that was nothing but an empty—

The door opened.

He looked so different with his own home as a background behind him. Older. Worn down. He tried to smile but it faded from his lips before it could take proper hold. "Tina."

"Don't panic." She held up the wine. "I just want to give you these."

He didn't say anything, didn't invite her in out of the cold (ha!) but he moved outside a little and pulled the door to behind him.

"I'm not going to cause a scene or anything," Tina said, hating that even in that stupid Christmas-knit jumper she still wanted him.

A voice called from inside.

"That the girl from the club?"

"Club? No. God, no. It's my wife."

He was good enough to wince, at least.

Tina gritted her teeth but managed, "Tell her I'm a charity case or something."

"You weren't a charity case," he said, and she hated herself even more for the warm feeling it gave her.

"Really?" She felt tears coming and tried to smile them away.

Jake satisfied himself that the door was shut enough and came out onto the front step. "Really," he said. He pointed to where a single stub of mistletoe hung in the porch then took her face in his hands and kissed her, albeit briefly. "Merry Christmas."

Tina stepped closer and kissed him again, more urgently, more passionately, and after a stunned moment and a brief noise of protest, Jake returned it. She felt his tongue and welcomed it, but then felt something else. A leaf. Several leaves. They spread from his mouth to fill hers. Tendrils pushed their way past her teeth, wrapped her tongue, and plunged deep into her throat. She tried to pull away but still he kissed her. One hand even found her breasts, and when she groaned she only offered him more room to fill. Her mouth was thick with leaves and berries, and still more pushed their way in. She could barely breathe.

Jake broke away from the kiss, panting for breath that Tina still couldn't take. He said quietly, "I'll see you later, yeah?"

Tina could only nod. If she said anything she'd lose everything he'd given her. She tried to swallow all of it down as he smiled goodbye and closed the door.

*

Jake's wife came into the hall with two steaming plates of food. "Who was it?" she asked.

Jake closed the door and hoped the redness in his face could be put down to the cold outside. "Someone from work." Then, to distract her from other questions, to draw her attention elsewhere, he raised the bottles and said, "They brought a Christmas present."

"Mm, nice. Red and white." She carried the plates through to the dining room. "Which one shall we have with dinner?"

"Hell," he said, following her, "It's Christmas. Let's drink them both."

TURTLEDOVE

Every Christmas Eve we go down to the bridge to throw our presents into the river. Nobody likes doing it, especially me, but we always do. One year Aunt Sally got out of it by being in Australia but the family always talk about it so she wishes she never had. Granddad, too, got out of it once because he was in hospital but nobody could blame him for that. It was far too cold to get a man his age out in the ice-sharp air. Otherwise, we all of us go down, every late December, woolly-layered and thickly-packed in jackets and coats. Gloves are a must because there'll be no plunging hands into pockets, nor is there much chance of heating them with breath because we'll each be carrying something ribbon-wrapped and parcelled-pretty. Our gift to the river.

I've already chosen this year's. It sits beneath the tree, leaning against the plastic clamp-stand and held in place by a rosette on the present underneath. It's the standard shoebox shape; all of them are, regardless of what's inside. We're not supposed to know what we give, you see—it has to be ours, that's all. If we knew, we'd all give away the socks or the toiletries probably, but this way we might be giving up our main present and that would really mean something. One year, my Auntie Ruth cast a string of pearls into the water. She didn't know until Uncle David told her Christmas Day, looking drawn and forlorn at the sparkly litter and empty boxes around them and wondering at the luck of it all. Personally, I believe he lied about the pearls. She probably lost a gift-set of pens or something.

Lost.

People think it's my fault we do this. They think Gem fell

because I wasn't watching but the truth of it is I saw the whole thing. I even tried to stop her but nobody would ever believe that so I don't tell them. I don't think any of them suppose I did anything deliberately, their opinion of me isn't so low as that. No, they just think I wasn't paying attention. I was, because she'd said, "Look at me!" as she walked the handrail, arms out for balance. She faked a wobble, dramatic theatrics, and straightened with a laugh, but it was the straightening out that got her. She stepped down on a frozen spot and though she flapped her arms like wings her feet slid out from beneath her and then... well, then she was gone.

The river was frozen that year, so it was a sharp crack! that broke the silence of that frosty afternoon, followed by my cry. I ran to the rails and looked down. It's not a long fall from the bridge, I remember thinking. And, she'll be all right. She has to be all right. We'll be all right.

And she was - for a moment. She lay there, stunned, looking up at a sky with me in it looking down, and she began to laugh. Then the ice split apart and folded up and she went under—whoosh! — engulfed in a frothy splash that took her breath and mine.

Now there's just one of us. Half of what mum and dad gave the world. I see her, still, in every mirror, her ghost and mine at the same time, and even if I say "Look at me!" all I do is show people, "Here is how she would have looked now: my sister; my twin". My mother loves me differently for it while my father loves me twice as much as if to compensate. As if I am both.

Sometimes I feel like I am. Not like before, not both together, but separately; me to me, but forever her to them. Gem and I torn apart, but not by the river.

Still, it's the river that gets her gifts. The idea had been to get us through the first Christmas without her but it accidentally became tradition. Like buying cheap crackers for shit toys no one will play with, or inviting people to a dinner you don't really want to eat, let alone cook, while those you miss and want with you most can never come for dinner even though you'd cook anything for them, anything at all, and it wouldn't matter how crappy the crackers were as long as you had someone to pull them with.

Instead there is a chair with no one there, me sitting beside it, the ghost of a Christmas past between us.

I get up very early Christmas Day. Loads of kids do, I know. But I'm not such a kid any more, and yet I'm up before the sun, before any surprised Santa-parent or gift-giddy child. I go to the river. I know where most of the presents wash up, you see. It's not far from where Gemma was found, blue-skinned and river-chilled. Thinking of how we wrapped her up, thinking of the box we put her in and the tree we buried her under, thinking of when I reached for her and pushed when I should have pulled, I feel like it's me who fell, me who was lost and boxed up in darkness. I gather up the gifts cast in her wake and I hide them away, under the bridge where so much water has passed. Then I return home.

When the New Year comes I will sell the presents meant for her and I will buy things I like, things she would have liked. I will wrap them neatly, corners folded tight and crisp, and I will offer them to the place where she'll always be – the silver stretch of river by the bridge. Maybe one year it will be ice again and she can be with me. We could sit surrounded by double the gifts I've ever received, mine on the ground and hers in the water not getting wet, mere ghosts of Christmas presents, and we can open them together, exactly together, and afterwards, staring at the gifts for what they really are, I will see my sister looking up to see the world with me in it and we will wonder which of us is frozen.

HANS

Hans usually enjoyed road trips, especially late at night in the snow. He liked the quiet hush of the engine, the shush of the tyres on the wet streets. Father played the radio low, little more than a murmur. Something local with lots of talking. A comforting sound. Hans could doze in the back of the car just as comfortably as in his bed at home. Better, thanks to the gentle rumble of the engine and the careful way Father drove. It was cold outside, nearly Christmas, so the heater was on as well, adding to the background hum, filling the car with a snug warmth so that Hans barely needed the blanket draped over him. He tried to watch the scenery as it passed, the dark lines of pines beside the autobahn, but the warmth of the car and its steady motion made his eyelids heavy. He didn't mind. He liked the dreamy quality it gave everything as they drove.

It had taken Hans a while to get used to all the travelling. Father was a sales representative, an area manager, and it meant he was always on the move. That used to be okay because Hans would stay with Mother, but now Hans had to come too. Sometimes he couldn't because of school, and that made things awkward for Father, but often he went along anyway. He liked to imagine he was learning the job, that he would take over from Father one day, travelling the country in his own car. Maybe even beyond the country; this was Europe, and you could drive almost anywhere. Father was all the way from England. It would be good to go there.

Hans usually enjoyed road trips. Usually. But during this one his comfortable doze couldn't hold him for very long and he kept waking from it. Father was singing the same song whenever he woke, something in English. It was called "Driving Home For Christmas".

"Are we nearly there?" Hans asked. He'd asked a few times because asking about where they were going got him no answer at all.

"Nearly."

At some point they had come off the autobahn and the lines of government-planted trees had become the outskirts of actual forest. The dark shape of it passed in upright smudges of ghostly shadow, black at the trunks but white in the branches where snow had gathered. At the side of the road the snow was a dirty slush, blackened and foul, but in the boughs of the trees it was still bright and fresh, sparkling occasionally in the beams of headlights. Hans could easily imagine the light catching the eyes of wolves in there, making them glow like embers in a dying fire. Once, all of this area had been wild and wolves had passed through the countryside and its woodland. Stalking deer, maybe. Maybe even reindeer, this time of year.

"Watch out, Rudolph," Hans muttered. With his nose so bright, Rudolph would have been easy prey for wolves. Hans had always liked Rudolph. He wondered if the reindeer, unable to play with the others, would have cared about a wolf or two and decided yes, he probably would.

"What did you say?"

Father's voice was sharper than it usually was. Maybe he was stressed. Hans didn't know his Father very well because he was always working away, and though his bond with Mother had been strong, sometimes he felt he barely knew this man. Maybe it was work that had him so stressed. Maybe it was the time of year.

Christmas could be very hard for some people, Hans knew, and now Mother was gone, so…

"Hans?"

"Just talking to myself."

He tried to get his sleepiness back but it refused. He was waking up, curious about the woods, the destination, thinking of wolves and Father's stress and where they might be going. The inside of the car no longer felt snug. He rubbed the crusts of sleep from his eyes and sat up properly.

The logo of a petrol station lit up the night ahead and Father began to slow. Hans heard the steady tick, tick, tick, of the indicator and they began to pull over. The fuel gauge said they still had nearly three quarters but Hans was getting to know Father's habits now; he didn't like to dip beneath half because he had a fear of getting stuck.

"Look, Hans. Christmas lights."

The station had draped the windows of its store with strings of multicoloured lights and they blinked off and on and ran in flashing patterns. A bright Santa Claus bent down with a neon present, then stood again with it.

"Yeah."

Hans was too old for something like that to excite him, and he wasn't sure he liked it really anyway. Santa looked like he was giving something away then taking it back again. Or taking something and giving it back. It felt familiar and he wondered if he'd seen it before.

"Five minutes," Father said, getting out of the car. He did it quick, door open just long enough for the dashboard to announce it once, bing!, but a lot of the heat was still snatched out of the car. Or a lot of the cold leapt in quick. Hans brought the blanket up around him again and saw his breath frost briefly before the temperature balanced out.

Outside, Father was watching the numbers turning on the pump. Even though they were climbing higher they reminded Hans of a countdown. He tried to imagine the countdown was to blast off, the car a rocketship on its way to new places, but he kept thinking of a bomb waiting to explode.

Flakes of snow fell slowly outside, rested on the window, and melted. Hans watched them, watched the drops run down the glass until another car pulled in. It was a large car, a family one, and it was full. There were only two children in the back but the other seats were filled with parcels wrapped in colourful paper and tied with elaborate bows. Hans thought of Santa taking them back. For a moment Hans thought one of the children, the boy, was pointing at him. He wasn't, though. He was drawing pictures on the misted glass of his window. The girl beside him was showing something in a magazine to Mother who was turned around in her seat to see. She was smiling.

Hans smiled too, trying to be happy for the girl, and for the boy, but he still felt sad as well.

The sudden sound of the driver's door opening startled him but Father didn't notice. "All set," he said, slamming the door shut. The car rocked slightly as he settled back into his seat. He didn't start the engine right away. He breathed on his hands to warm them.

"Where are we going?" Hans asked. This time he hoped he wouldn't get an answer, though he wasn't sure why.

Father leant on the steering wheel and put his hands flat to his face for a moment, over his eyes. He rubbed, sighed, and sat up again.

"Father?"

The man winced. "Don't," he said. And, "It's a surprise." Hans could tell he regretted saying that but then the engine growled back to life and they were off again.

The noise of the car didn't settle into its usual purr. To Hans the engine sounded loud now, and the shush of each passing car was more like a hiss. Not that there were many other cars out here, not compared to the autobahn.

"It's snowing," Hans said, just to say something. He leant forward to watch it. Far away from the car the snow fell slowly, gently, but on the road it moved fast, swept into flurries in the wake of other vehicles. The car was warming up again.

"It won't last," Father said.

Hans tried to focus on the slow snow instead of the fast but it was difficult. He watched it settle in the trees, disappearing amongst the rest of the snow or melting into glistening black bark, never to be seen again.

Someone watched them from the tree line. Hans saw them, just for a moment, as they passed. He thought it was a small snowman at first because it was so encrusted with snow but it raised a hand. Hello, maybe. Or stop. Then it was behind them.

Hans turned quickly in his seat and looked back but it was gone, already swallowed up by the dark.

"I just saw someone."

"Hm?"

"In the trees. In the snow."

"Maybe you did."

They drove on in quiet for a moment. At the side of the road a sign came up, came up, came up, and went past. Hans couldn't make out the writing because it was a wooden sign and not a proper reflective one and it went by too quickly, but he saw the dim shape of an arrow painted on it.

"Did they look like they were in trouble?"

Hans was looking behind them again but the sign was gone.

"The person you saw, Hans. Had they broken down? Were they stuck?"

"No," said Hans. "It was a child, I think."

"A child?"

"I couldn't see if it was a boy or a girl."

They were slowing.

"Where are we going?"

Another sign was coming up. Hans didn't want to see it. The indicator was tick-tick-ticking like a countdown and they pulled into a slower lane, ready to turn away from one road into another.

"They wouldn't let kids play out this late," Father said. He said it as they turned, distracted by the manoeuvre. "Not in the woods. Not so close to the road."

"Who wouldn't?"

But Hans knew. A string of white lights had been clipped around the next sign and Hans saw it quite clearly. He recognised the picture and he recognised the name.

"No."

"Just for a little while."

"No, Father!"

"Don't call me that. I told you not to call me that."

Hans unbuckled his seatbelt as if to throw himself out of the car, but they were already stopping.

Hans didn't want to but he began to cry. "I hate it here."

"Hans. Please."

Hans may not have known the man well, but he knew the stare

he was getting in the mirror. He looked away from it and was quiet.

Cold flooded the car, rushing in through the driver's door. The man who was not Father, not really, opened the door for Hans as well and the last of the warmth vanished, thinned by the cold air and transformed into chill. Hans put on his jacket. He considered running but even getting out of the car he slipped on the icy ground. He wouldn't make it very far.

The man gripped Hans by the arm to steady him but did not let go afterwards. He held him all the way to the orphanage doors. He didn't let go until they were inside.

*

"You can't just return him, Mr Stevens. You can't just drop in, without an appointment, at Christmas, and deposit him back where you got him from."

"I understand that, but—"

"You have a responsibility now."

"I know, but—"

"There were forms."

Father — Mr Stevens — said something in English, something angry, then, "Of course there were forms, there are always forms."

Hans was looking into the recreation room. His arm hurt from where Fa — Mr Stevens — had gripped it. Hans rubbed his arm and watched the children gathered in the other room beside a coal fire, sitting in a semi-circle before a small television. They were watching other children visit Father Christmas in a pretend grotto, ushered in one at a time by a woman dressed as an elf.

Hans couldn't hear the television properly but every time the child on Santa's knee asked for something Santa looked awkward and flustered and the audience laughed. Sometimes the orphans watching laughed too but it sounded like they were copying what they heard instead of really laughing and they didn't do it often.

"Mr Stevens, I don't know what you expect..."

Hans tuned the adults out to focus on the television and its laughter, but the more he tried to listen the more the laughter sounded cruel. He thought again of that neon Santa at the petrol station.

One of the children was watching Hans instead of the screen. She was chewing on the hair of her blonde ponytail. She raised a hand to wave, slowly, but without a smile. Hans returned it. He didn't recognise any of them. He didn't think it was because they were new. He thought it was because he'd decided to forget. Not that his time here had been awful. Nobody hurt him or anything. It was just... empty. Empty time. A world on pause, and lonely. The orphanage was a place to wait, and wait, and be disappointed.

"Well, we can argue all day or you can just take him."

"Mr Stevens!"

"I have to go."

For a moment it seemed like there'd been a change of plan because Hans was turned around, steered by a strong grip on his shoulder. Then the hand was gone as his father-not-father moved to open the door and the cold came in, a gust of snow that made Hans blink and squint. His not-father disappeared into it and was gone and Hans stood alone in the hall facing a closed door.

"Hans, dear thing, are you all right?"

The woman that had been angry a moment ago was now pretending to be soft and kind and warm. She squatted down beside him. Hans wiped his eyes. He had snow in them. "He hurt me," he said.

"Mr Stevens?"

Hans nodded. He rolled up his sleeve and showed her where he knew there'd be bruises. The woman sighed her sympathy and said, "Did he do this to you?" Hans couldn't remember if he knew this woman from before or just wanted to. He nodded.

"Did he do anything else?"

Hans cried. He didn't want to, but he couldn't help it. "He hurt me," he said again. And then he said a lot of things that weren't true. Sitting on the man's knee, giving, taking. He didn't want to say these things but he couldn't help it, he was upset. The woman looked like she wanted to cry too and she gave him a tight hug that wasn't soft or kind or warm because her uniform was stiff and smelled too clean. Hans could tell she was trying, though.

"Let's get you a bed," she said. "We'll talk about this again tomorrow. I need to call someone first, all right Hans?"

Hans wanted Mother even though she wasn't really his mother but she was gone now so no, Hans was not all right.

He nodded anyway.

*

Running was difficult not because the snow was deep but because it had been trodden into ice around the building and his feet slid-slipped as he tried to hurry. He still hurried though, hands out at his sides, until eventually he was on the grass where the snow was fresh and he was held a little by his own footprints. He made for the darkening between the trees and there he hunkered down to catch his breath. It puffed from him in little clouds of frost.

The orphanage was quiet. Some of the windows were still lit and occasionally Hans saw someone moving around inside but no one was coming out to shout or chase him. Nobody was even looking. He thought maybe if it was snowing there'd be a face at the window to watch, but it wasn't snowing anymore. It was cold, though. He had his coat but it wasn't very thick and it didn't stay waterproof for long – it wasn't that kind of coat. His good one was at home. Or where home used to be. Or maybe it was still in the car in the bag of clothes he took around with him when Father was working and on the road. Hans wished he was in the car right now. He wanted the snuggled warmth of the back seat and the soft drone of the radio. The shadows in the woods were cold and staying still was making him colder.

Hans turned away from the building and considered the deeper woods behind him. There was no such thing as wolves anymore (not here anyway, only in zoos) and he was too old to believe in spookier things like ghosts or witches, but he watched the news and he knew that monsters were real and some of them liked the woods.

He ran into the trees anyway.

At first they were positioned an equal distance apart in parallel lines, but eventually they began to bunch up and cluster, as if whoever had planted them had given up on neatness and order. By the time he noticed, Hans could no longer hear the quiet hiss of passing cars nearby. He had intended to use the traffic sound for his bearings, but somewhere along the way he had forgotten to listen out for the autobahn and now it was lost and so was he.

It didn't matter. If he became really lost he could always follow his own tracks back, though he hoped he wouldn't have to. As long as his prints remained clear he should be—

Hans spotted other tracks in the snow alongside his. They were small split circles, like those of a deer maybe. Sometimes, looking back, it seemed as if the deer feet became human ones but it was just his shoeprints treading over some of the circles where the tracks crissed-and-crossed. He liked the patterns they made entwined. Ahead there was only one set. He would add his prints to those as well; he had no other course to guide him, so he followed the trail into the fading light.

*

The trail didn't meander much at all except where the foliage became too dense to pass through, the woods thickening with bushes and briars. Hans had to pick his way between tangles of brambled vine and around coarse stumps of ice-sparkled shrubbery. He was concentrating so much on this, and on keeping the tracks in sight, that it wasn't until the snow brightened with moonlight that Hans looked up to see the trees had thinned around him and he stood in a clearing, crisp and dazzling and open to the night sky. The ground was plump with fallen snow.

And there were snowmen. Lots and lots of snowmen, gathered in a mismatched crowd as if each was a stranger to the other. Some looked to have been there a while, frozen into shapes that shone their silver light from solid ice, but one looked fresh; the ground around it had been swept into long shallow arcs where handfuls of snow had been gathered up for building. Some of the snowmen wore hats. Some had scarves. One had a bright plastic handbag pressed into its side, its branch-arm threaded through the strap. Another had a bonnet like from the olden days. All of them had eyes of stone and semi-circle smiles, grins of coal so dark it seemed the night had split their faces. All of them were small, not snowmen but snowchildren, boys and girls.

"You're from the orphanage."

Hans was startled. He hadn't noticed the girl, either because he was distracted by the snowchildren or because she looked like one herself; her jacket was snow-crusted and the hat she wore pulled down over her blonde hair was made of white wool. Her cheeks were pink though, and she puffed little clouds from her mouth when she spoke. "I remember you," she said. "From before. Have you come to get me?"

"No," Hans said. "I'm running away."

"Me too. Obviously." She pushed red berries into one of the snowheads. "It's supposed to look like lipstick. Does it look like lipstick?"

"A bit. But you're pushing them too far."

"You can help if you want."

Hans didn't say anything. He didn't move. He looked at all of the snowmen and snowwomen. The snowboys and snowgirls.

"My name's Gertrude but I hate it and everyone calls me Trudy."

He waited a while before finally saying, "My name's Hans."

Trudy dug the berries free and began setting them back in place, arranging them carefully this time.

"Why don't you make any adults?" Hans asked her.

She looked at Hans like it was the stupidest question in the whole world. When Hans said nothing she said, "They'd melt anyway."

"Why don't the children ones melt?"

She pushed a branch into the snow heap before her, breaking off pieces and adjusting the angle so that the snowgirl looked like she was covering her mouth with a skinny hand. She shrugged. "They just don't," she said.

She stepped back from the snowgirl and assessed her work. "I'm not allowed to wear lipstick," she said. She put her hand over her mouth for a moment, touching her lips with gloved fingers and becoming a momentary reflection of what she had made. Then she took off her hat and fit it to the snowgirl's head, reshaping some of the snow to hold it in place. "When I had a mum, she said she'd teach me how to put it on when I was older and I'm older now."

She began unwinding the scarf from around her neck.

"You'll get cold," Hans said.

"Not for long, though." She walked a circle around the snowgirl, wrapping the scarf around a non-existent neck. She took off her gloves as well and put them over stick-fingers as best she could. "Anyway, you'll get cold too. You don't have a proper coat on, or gloves, or a scarf, or even a hat."

She was right. His hands were cold even in his pockets. Even under his armpits. He looked around at the snowchildren.

"Don't you dare," said Trudy. "You can't take theirs."

"Why not?"

"All right, you can only take it if its yours. Which one is yours?"

"What do you mean?"

Trudy pointed at the snowchildren, sweeping her arm around in a gesture to encompass all of them. "Which one did you make to get away?"

"None of them."

The girl scowled at him.

"I didn't make any of the stupid snowmen."

Trudy crossed her arms over her chest. "That's why you're back," she said. "You're not very nice."

"Neither are you, Gertrude." Hans plunged his hands back into his pockets and cut across the clearing with his head down. He zig-zagged back and forth, looking at the snow.

"What are you looking for? Hey, where are you going?"

Hans had found the tracks again. He followed them to the edge of the clearing, his shoulders hunched against the cold. He walked quickly.

"Where are you going?"

But suddenly Hans wasn't going anywhere. He'd seen something move. A shadow moved amongst shadows in the gloom ahead of him.

"Hans—"

"Ssh!"

There was a rustle in the foliage, the quiet crack and shiver of twigs breaking, leaves shaking. Hans held his breath, one foot still raised ready for his next step. "There's a deer," he said.

He could only see some of it. Part of its body was dappled with moonlight, its tawny flank spotted silver-grey. Its head was down in the dark, feeding at something low or catching a scent, but it moved slowly forward with barely any sound, only the ghostly whisper of falling snow as leaves brushed against leaves and the soft fur of its hide.

Trudy was coming to see as well. Hans could hear the slow scrunch, scrunch, of snow trodden flat beneath her boots as she approached. Each sound was drawn out as she tried to be quiet. Hans held his arm out behind to tell her stop and she did, but she said, "What is it?" with a voice hushed to near silence.

Hans was about to tell her when the creature raised its head and the breath he'd prepared to whisper with came out as a gasp.

The first thing he saw was its eyes. It had taken another step forward as it raised into view and that had brought a wash of silver light over its head, neck, and torso. The light gleamed from large dark eyes, black and round like a deer's but much bigger, and set in a face that was wrong. The face was long like a deer's but fleshed and featured in a way that was human. The nose... the nose descended from beneath the eyes, drawn down to a mouth that was something like a muzzle without fur, just freckled skin and a small mouth that chewed at the leaves protruding from between thin lips. As Hans watched, it dipped its head again to the bushes and took another mouthful of leaves, tugging at the twigs as it straightened, stripping them bare and shaking snow loose in soft cloudfalls. She had long wild tangled hair, swept back from the face and littered with twigs and leaves. It was definitely a she, Hans realised. He could see her breasts and he was embarrassed by their nakedness. Large and heavy, they sloped from a chest that looked smooth and tawny-tanned but was furred in the middle, a triangle of it fanning out from between the breasts into a full pelt at her waist and beyond.

"What is it?" Trudy asked again, so quiet that Hans only heard her because he wasn't breathing. "I can't see."

Hans didn't know what it was. It, she, had taken a few more cautious steps closer as she chewed her leaves and he could see more now. Occasionally she picked and ate berries, plucking them from bushes with human hands and bringing them to her mouth with slender arms as bare as the rest of her human skin but spotted with large freckles. Her lower body was all deer, fur-thatched from the waist down to well-muscled thighs and calves that seemed to angle backwards. Her feet were hooves, tiny hooves; Hans saw them when they lifted from the snow. They never would have supported her properly except that she had four of them, body stretching out behind to a firm rump and two more legs. He couldn't see if there was a tail.

She made a gentle mewling sound. Hans looked into that strange face again and she raised her arms to him.

Trudy said, "Hans, move."

The deerwoman bobbed her head down and sideways; come on, come on.

Hans took a step closer. Cautiously at first. Slowly. But she mewled again, beckoning him with both hands to come, and her small mouth seemed to smile with thin black lips, so Hans went to her. He raised his own arms and reached his hands towards hers and she nodded encouragement. She even crouched a little because she was taller, bending at the waist and leaning on her forelegs. Hans was close enough to see her fur was lighter in places, not with snow but patches of colour. And then his hands were in hers and hers were warm and strong. They gripped him tight and pulled him close to her so suddenly that he slipped a little but she held him easily and he did not fall. She gathered him close and Hans could smell the musky scent of her fur as she pressed his face to her body in a firm full hug. She held him at the back with one arm and tried to cradle him. She used her other hand to guide his head, turning his face to press him to her nipple, but Hans turned his head away. It only made her pull him tighter and for a moment he feared she'd smother him. She didn't quite have the strength to lift him, though she tried, so as she struggled with his face she pushed her chest to his mouth. He felt the nipple at his lips, soft and wet, and eventually he had no choice but to suckle there.

Trudy gasped behind him and Hans was suddenly released, dropping to the cold ground as he lost his balance. The deerwoman was startled into a series of skittish sidesteps and long ears Hans hadn't noticed twitched in her matted hair. Hans reached for her from where he lay but she only blinked her large glassy dark eyes and backed away with a bleating sound. Then she turned tail (she did have a tail, Hans saw the white upright puff of it) and she ran, carried away swiftly on four legs that kicked up flurries of snow as she fled.

"Wait!" Hans cried. He scrambled clumsily to his feet, snow filling his clothes and chilling his skin.

"Wait!" echoed Trudy.

Hans ran.

The deerwoman was bounding ahead in short bursts of speed that zigged and zagged, springing one way and then the other as she dodged obstacles Hans couldn't see. She was leading him further into the woods. The darkness was deeper here yet Hans was able to leap over things, duck under things, by following. He often slipped and stumbled, falling and getting up again all at once, and frequently he felt the whip of branches across his face and brambles tearing at his clothes, but what he had tasted was rich and thick and warm and he wanted more. What he had felt was soft and gentle and warm and he wanted that as well.

Hans was crying as he ran. His tears were cold on his cheeks. He tried to call after her but the name he wanted to use couldn't get past the taste in his mouth and she pulled further and further away from him until eventually, exhausted, he collapsed into a drift of snow that almost covered him. He lay there, panting. He tried to hug himself warm, but the snow blanket was comforting too in its own way. He wanted to sleep. He wanted to close his eyes and wake up in Father's car. He wanted—

"Mother."

The forest stirred. This time it was the fast snap-and-crack of something moving quickly, something coming right at him from the way he had come, pushing through bushes and branches at speed. Hans felt the ground beneath him thunder.

He stood and shook the snow from his clothes. He thought of wolves and was not frightened. He waited to see their coal-ember eyes coming for him in the dark and when the shadows trembled and parted Hans opened his arms to whatever came.

But it was Trudy's laughter that came at him. The crash and trample of the woodland sounded far too big for her and yet it was her laughter, her fits of breathy giggles and her cries of delight, that rushed towards him, towards him, in the silver dark.

What burst from the foliage though was a magnificent stag.

"Hans!" Trudy cried.

She was clinging to the creature. Hans saw her held in strong arms, cradled against a firm chest that was muscled and full-furred and scarred, a flash of detail caught in a moonbeam as the man-deer rushed past. Trudy had her arms around the creature's thick neck. Its head was bent low, thrust forward, and she clutched at antlers that emerged from human hair, a wide spread of horns carrying broken twigs and leaves like Christmas decorations. It leapt past Hans, carried high on huge legs that seemed more horse than deer, and the gust of breeze that came with its passing carried the musky smell of its flanks, the whiff of its sweat-wet fur. A glimpse was all, and then they were past him, a flexing rump and something large dangling between, disappearing back into the dark, swallowed again by the woods. Gone.

His name trailed behind with the last of Trudy's laughter and Hans was left standing with open arms.

He lowered them slowly. He wouldn't chase after them, they were moving too fast anyway, but he thought he knew what he had to do.

*

The other children watched as Hans finished his task, a semi-circle audience around the edge of the clearing as silent as the falling snow they were made from. Hans did not have gloves, or a scarf, or even a hat, but he dressed his snowchild as best he could. He gave it his thin coat. He took off his shoes as well and pressed them into where his mound of snow met the ground. He found two suitable branches for arms and he pushed these into each side, open wide, and he pressed stones into the face for eyes. He didn't have any coal for the mouth so he scooped it hollow and tried to pretend it wasn't screaming.

He sat down in the snow beside it, shivering, and wondered who would find him.

SNOWBOOKS HORROR NOVELLAS

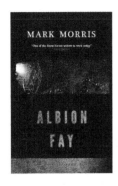

ALBION FAY

Mark Morris

Albion Fay, a holiday house in the middle of nowhere, surrounded by nature's bounty. For the adults, a time for relaxation and to recharge the batteries, while for the children, a chance for exploration and adventure in the English countryside.

A happy time for all: nothing could possibly go wrong. Or could it? What should be a magical time ends in tragedy – but what really happened that summer?

SCOURGE

Gary Fry

Felachnids: a race of mythical creatures that are rumoured to live in the dark Yorkshire countryside.

The yellow eyes, the double-jointed limbs, the heads that turned backwards whenever that was necessary. These creatures, which otherwise resembled humans, appeared to occupy a small village in North Yorkshire called Nathen.

And Lee Parker is determined to track them down.

SNOWBOOKS HORROR NOVELLAS

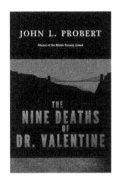

THE NINE DEATHS OF DR VALENTINE

John L. Probert

Someone is killing doctors in the style of the murders in Vincent Price movies, leaving the Bristol police baffled. The only man who could possibly be responsible died years ago... or did he... ?

The police in Bristol have been confronted by a series of the most perplexingly elaborate deaths they've ever encountered in all their years of murder enquiries. The only thing which connects them is their seemingly random nature and their sheer outrageousness. As Detective Inspector Longdon and his assistant Sergeant Jenny Newham (with the help of pathologist Dr. Richard Patterson) race against time to find the murderer, they eventually realise that the link which connects the killings is even more bizarre than any of them dared to think....

www.snowbooks.com